TALES OF YESTERDAY'S TOMORROW

RICH WINTERSTETTER

FOR BELLS

His passion for stories and writing (and eggs) made him
fun to talk to.
His genuine care for people and overall personal
excellence made him a friend.

I miss you buddy.

CONTENTS

ACKNOWLEDGMENTS

Writing a novel is a one man job.
Publishing one takes a small village - even if it is "only" republishing your previous work as an anthology.

So my eternal thanks to Hambo, Lisa and Mikey - for your direct input and help, making either this entire thing or parts of it reality.

Big thanks also goes to Elcin, Manu, Bells, Jonathan, Mo, Marco and Felix - for providing feedback in the past (and hopefully also in the future).

And last but not least, thank you to my parents for raising me around books and encouraging me to read and write growing up. Look what you have done!

THE FOREIGN EFFECT

PROLOGUE

The warm, damp air fogged up the inside of the bathroom window as the young blonde woman stopped the water pouring into the bathtub. Absentmindedly she stared into the tub as she swirled her fingers through the hot, rising water. She loosened her bathrobe and climbed in. She sat down and let the bath engulf her almost completely. As the foam of the bath salts tickled her chin, the woman closed her green eyes and submerged her head for a second. She came back up and brushed her hair out of her face. Settling down, she breathed in the aromatic fumes. She had always liked a good, hot, relaxing bath. It helped her clear her mind. The woman reached for a glass of red wine, which was standing on a small side table next to the tub. She sipped on it, and her gaze wandered towards the ceiling of the elegantly furnished bathroom. Her free hand resting on her thigh, the woman chuckled – a sad, cynical chuckle – as she let her fingers run over her smooth young skin. "Who would have thought it would come to this?" The woman awkwardly wrapped her fingers around the wineglass and squeezed them until it shattered, cutting herself as it disintegrated in her palm. But the woman did not flinch. With childlike amazement, she watched as the red wine mixed itself with her blood and ran down her forearm. She got hold of a big and sharp shard of the glass and turned it, the light reflecting in its surface as well as the wet blood stains on it, and chuckled again. She had lived a long life, but even in her darkest moments she never thought she'd find herself in this situation. An old soul in a young body. Tears started to form in those beautiful green eyes of hers, and for once she didn't fight them. Quietly sobbing, her voice breaking, she started to hum the melody of "What a Difference a Day Makes" as she slowly moved the shard towards her wrist.

CHAPTER I

Rebecca stumbled into the bathroom and desperately slammed the toilet seat against the water pipes, immediately puking savagely and violently down the bowl. Two wet belches and a couple of dry heaves later, she flushed the remains of her breakfast down the drain, trying her best to ignore the lingering taste of bile in her mouth. Turning around to the sink she couldn't help but catch a look in the mirror. Brown eyes looked back at her under a sweaty brow. She was exhausted, and not only because of what just happened. Rebecca washed her hands and splashed her face with cold water while trying not to think of the bucket. She fixed her black hair back into a ponytail and looked directly into her reflection's eyes, trying to force her body to move. To go back to the kitchen and the bucket. "C'mon! You have to go to work. You can't afford to act like a little spoiled brat," she uttered, speaking through clenched teeth. "Handle it! Take control of the situation!" Rebecca repeated her mother's favorite phrase. Repeating it in her head over and over, turning it into a mantra, steeling herself against what was to come. Rebecca took a deep breath and went back into the kitchen. She handled it. Ten minutes later, Rebecca kissed her mother goodbye. She was sleeping again. Rebecca was grateful for every hour her mother could rest. The bowel cancer kept her up and in pain more often than not, chewing at her, slowly eating away at the woman Rebecca had loved and looked up to all her life. Quietly closing the bedroom door, Rebecca checked her uniform for stains one last time and left the apartment.

"Hey Rebecca!" She jumped at the greeting of her neighbor Diana, also on her way to work. Diana was a shrink downtown and one of the few people in her apartment building Rebecca actually talked to. In fact, Diana had helped her out with her mother on several occasions, enough so that the two women could at least pretend to be friends. "Hey Diana. How are you?" Rebecca answered more out of programmed custom than actual interest. She fussed with the keycard to lock the apartment door. The other woman looked at her, giving her a professional shrink-like smile that somehow managed to feel genuine. "Everything okay with your mom?" Rebecca looked up and into Diana's green eyes. She paused for a second. "It's getting worse..." She surprised herself at how matter of fact she could put it. "I'm sorry," Diana retorted with the trained skill of a shrink making it sound like she actually was. But something was off. Rebecca couldn't put her finger on it, but she just got the feeling that Diana was not quite her usual charming, lovable self. Call it a cop's hunch. She looked tired for starters. Dark shadows under her eyes, her makeup was stale as if she hadn't brushed it up for some time, almost as if she hadn't slept. Diana seemed like she was stressed out, but even more suspicious: Her smile took a moment too long to flash. Her body language didn't ooze as much warmth as usual. Her eyes jumped a tad too quickly at every movement they registered. Diana felt like an imitation of herself. She was trying to act calm though, which roused Rebecca's suspicions even more. "What about you? Are YOU okay?" Diana looked at her. For a second it seemed like she was about to say something, but Rebecca could see the moment come and go in her neighbor's eyes. It was only a fraction of a second before the shrink found her mask again and flashed Rebecca a bright, phony smile. "Why yes, Officer Gonzalez. Everything is fine!" Rebecca took the hint to mind her own business and said goodbye as they exited the apartment building.

Diana entered the garage, just to emerge moments later in her fancy dark-blue Tesla. Bitterly, Rebecca thought back to the days when she owned a car. Never something fancy like a Tesla, but that shitty old Ford of hers. She had bought it back in high school after saving up money for an eternity. The car was old to begin with, and after a decade of heavy usage it finally broke down. Rebecca didn't have the money to fix it – let alone buy a new car. She spat out on the boardwalk, still tasting the morning's events in her mouth. Her mind went from not being able to afford a car to unpaid medical bills, then back to the bucket – all within the couple of minutes it took her to walk to the bus stop.

Her cell phone started ringing in her pocket. Rebecca touched the chip in her left index finger with her thumb, closing the circuit and activating the small speaker implanted in her eardrum to take the call instead of actually using the phone. "Hey beaner baby. How are you?" Rebecca could hear her partner's voice just as if he was standing next to her. "What's up on your end of the rainbow motherfucker?" she answered, her voice getting picked up by another small chip near her larynx. "Just wanted to check in. As usual the duty roster for this week hasn't been updated yet. So are you coming in today? Or is it another siesta for you? Should I pick you up from the border wall?" "Thanks for asking Paul but I'm fine. I'm stopping by 'The Place' today first. I'll be done around noon!" "'The Place' again huh?" Paul's cheery tone vanished in an instant. Both of them said nothing for a while, an awkward silence growing between them. "What are you going to give them this time?" "None of your fucking business Paul!" Rebecca's answer was a bit harsher than she had intended. Despite their banter she was still on edge, and Paul had this way of being overly intimate for a colleague sometimes. Hell even for a friend. It made her uncomfortable and it didn't help that she hated having to go to "The Place" after all. Again their conversation paused awkwardly. Rebecca forced her voice back to a friendlier tone. "Can you pick me up around noon at Sirona?" she asked. Paul sighed. "Yeah sure. Bye!" He ended the call. "Que te folle un pez!" Rebecca swore. She was more mad at herself than at Paul, but at the moment he was an easier target.

 A couple of minutes later the bus finally arrived. After riding half an hour in the overly crowded sauna also referred to as public transportation, featuring air conditioning which had long ago surrendered to the summer weather and various flavors of bodily odor, she arrived at the headquarters of Sirona Corp in the heart of the city. The skyscraper was the dominant part of the skyline, and it's elegant but futuristic design, mixing glass windows and white ceramic panels, had become the number one motive for tourist merchandise – given the impact the company who owned it had on society. Back in the day it would have been featured on almost every postcard, but who sends postcards anymore these days? There wasn't even a mail service around nowadays. Rebecca was sure the building graced its fair share of unique and one of a kind social media profiles though. She rolled her eyes. She was in a special mood today. Making her way across Sirona Square, Rebecca passed tons of ads for "Memory Making" and "TransLife" and all the other services Sirona Corp offered. She had already blocked them all with her GPS ad blocker so they didn't start blasting in her face as soon as she came close to the billboards – an experience she was not too keen on reliving. She had made it almost to the main entrance when suddenly a pleasant female voice called out to her from her left. "Officer Rebecca Gonzalez! Have you ever dreamt of living in a past epoch? Sirona Corp offers a new stock of millennial memories! Remember the days! For only $9,99!" "Hijo de tu puta madre! How often do they put up new ones?" Rebecca pulled her phone out of her pocket, eager to silence the ad. "Stock limited. Monthly price. Billing begins thirty days after purchase and occurs monthly thereafter for a minimum of..." The ad suddenly came to a halt in the middle of the legal annotations the voice quickly rambled through. "There you go! Cállate puta!" Rebecca added it to her blocked list, actively fighting the urge to flip off the billboard. At least one thing she was in control of this morning! Sneering victoriously at the now silenced ad, she put her phone away and entered the building.

Already aware where she needed to go, Rebecca stood clear of the main reception desk and circled around to the back of the entry hall. She put her hand on a scanner next to a door that read "Personnel and Contractors Only!" and entered the door as soon as it unlocked. Rebecca found herself in a smaller hall with another reception desk and a busy young woman with red hair. "Hello Officer Gonzalez!" she said way too cheerfully. Rebecca couldn't remember ever having met the woman before. "How can I help you today?" "I was hoping to sell some more memories." Rebecca replied, slightly irritated by the overly good mood of the receptionist. "Sure thing Officer Gonzalez. Anything specific you were thinking of?" "Last time I was here, my mapping results showed two more memories that the company had an interest in." "If that's so they should still be in the system!" the receptionist squeaked and started punching numbers and characters into her keyboard. "Ah, there it is!" The squeaker stopped to look at her blank screen. Rebecca knew that the monitors throughout the building were there to avoid irritating older customers – the actual data being visible only to the receptionist on the screen in her glasses – but it still annoyed Rebecca because, out of habit, she started to look at the screen herself every time. It reminded her how much of this company was just decorum.

"One Class D memory of going skiing and a Class B… oooooh!" The receptionist looked at Rebecca with curious glee. "A Class B romantic memory. Content redacted," she continued in an overly theatrical tone. "Care to share the content of it?" She winked at Rebecca. "Listen!" Rebecca started massaging the bridge of her nose. "I had a really shitty day so far. So how about we skip the gossip and speed it up a bit?" The receptionist shot her a look that could have killed people. "Fine!" all traces of her overly cheery attitude vanished in an instant. "By the Sirona Corp guidelines I am obliged to inform you that should you enter an agreement over your memories, said memories will be erased from your mind forever. You will be compensated according to the agreement. Sirona Corp remains the right to refuse any and all refunds after the harvesting of the memory and takes no responsibility for eventual side effects like headaches, over-sensitivity to light and general unease. Do you agree to these terms?" The receptionist arched an eyebrow at Rebecca who just nodded. As usual, she felt a pang of guilt at the fact that the memories would be erased from her mind. During her first session she had asked the technician why Sirona was so keen on making sure her memories didn't stay with her. The answer was simple: It was best for business. That way, the memories Sirona sold were unique and rare. Plus, the deletion doubled as a sort of anti-piracy measure. If the original owner of the memory didn't have access to it anymore, they could not be sold again to unlicensed hacks and mindjackers, which kept the memories Sirona had in stock rare and the prices up. "The two memories would add up to a total of $139,99" the receptionist interrupted Rebecca's train of thought. "Did you adjust the prices again? Last time I got two hundred for just one Class B memory." "Our prices fluctuate with the amount of supply the company has access to, yes! So deal or no deal?"

Rebecca's mind flashed back to the day she spent with her mother skiing in Seattle. Back when it actually still snowed every once in a while. She allowed herself to take in the details of that specific memory for the very last time. She sighed. "I wish you guys would be interested in memories of me receiving astronomical medical bills! I could make a fortune with those. Let's do this!" She put her thumb on the scanner in front of her, signing the agreement, and the receptionist started punching keys on her keyboard again. "The agreed-upon amount has been wired to your bank account. Please go through the door to your right. Our personnel will be with you in a second!"

As Rebecca left the reception area, she could feel the glaring stare of the receptionist in her back. It didn't surprise her at all that she found she didn't care. The removal procedure itself was quick and efficient. Rebecca was taken into a small white room with something resembling a dentist's chair. The company was trying very hard to make the area not look like a hospital, despite the fact that they were performing the most invasive of procedures here. Apart from the chair, the whole scenery looked more like an office than an actual treatment room. One of the technicians put a small crown-like device on Rebecca's head and dosed her with a mixture of sedatives and contrast fluids. She spent half an hour in a drug-induced haze. When her head finally cleared back up again, the technician removed the head gear. Rebecca was handed a flier with all the "How to's" for possible side effects and aftercare of the procedure before she was dismissed. Less than an hour after she entered the building, Rebecca found herself back at Sirona Square. Just like after her previous trips to the "Memory Makers", she tried to remember what memories she had sold, fully aware of the fact that it was a useless endeavor. All she found was the indistinct feeling that something was missing, which would weaken over the next couple of days and eventually disappear completely.

As usual after she sold memories, Rebecca felt the first traces of a merciless headache starting in the back of her head. She was lucky though. Unlike most sellers, she didn't feel overly exhausted or disoriented. Neither did she have the more physical side effects like nose bleeds or uncontrolled vomiting. God knows she had enough throwing up for one day.

As Rebecca crossed Sirona Square, a car's horn honked at her from the street. Paul was waving towards her out of their patrol car's window as he awkwardly parked it halfway on the sidewalk. "Damn it you potato-humping Pot-Licker, you call that parking?" Rebecca said, picking up their usual tone of conversation. "Look who's talking? The spic! Do they even sell cars to you? Or do you just jack them?" He stepped out of the car with a big shit eating grin. Paul Killian was a pale, tall, skinny fella with short, reddish-brown hair worn in a way that tried to hide a receding hairline with little success. He was an F.B.I. – a Foreign Born Irish – and he looked the part. It was hard to find someone who was more the stereotypical Irishman than Paul. He was a leprechaun costume and a shillelagh shy of posing for a cereal box cover. Paul and Rebecca went to police academy together and had been partners for the last five years. More importantly: They were friends. Paul handed Rebecca a small brown paper bag. "Here!" She took the bag and grinned. "Potatoes?" - "Crystal meth! I might have topped it off with some aspirin." He shot her an apologetic glance and stretched his arms awkwardly. "I would have gotten you flowers, but I know you Latrinos are more into pills,"

She smiled warmly as they both got in the car. Rebecca popped two aspirin pills, and they both said nothing for a while. Just as Rebecca started up the car and signaled to move out of the parking spot, Paul blurted out "I'm sorry for earlier. It is none of my business. I just don't like that place, that's all!" He was looking at his shoes, like a small kid that got busted by his mother with one hand in the cookie jar. Rebecca shot him a quick glance as she drove down the street towards the precinct. "My morning was awful. I let it out on you. I'm sorry!" He smiled sadly. "Your mom?" "Yup!" "Anything I can help you with?" "Nope!" "Wanna talk about it?" Rebecca took another deep breath and sighed. "Remember that the doctors removed almost six feet of colon last month?" He nodded. "Well she threw up this morning, and when I went to clean the bucket it smelled of…" Rebecca felt a knot form in the back of her throat. She swallowed hard. "Feces. She is throwing up shit Paul. Cojeme… how is anyone… mierda!" A single tear was running down her cheek as she tried to find the right words. Paul graciously looked away. "Now don't throw that beaner slang at me. I thought you Hics were used to throwing up. God knows what you put in those burritos. Bean paste my ass!" Rebecca looked at Paul and they both started laughing.. "I swear to God, the chimichanga I had for dinner yesterday was daring me to get food poisoning. Oooh, you too weak ese! Me no potato senior!" Paul squeaked in a high-pitched bad latino accent. They giggled. A small cathartic giggle. Rebecca couldn't help but notice though how quickly her smile faded.

They drove in silence for a while. "You know." Rebecca finally broke the silence. "I find myself wishing for her to die. End her suffering… or at least that's what I tell myself." Another pause. "I just… don't think I can do this anymore. I'm tired. I'm spent. And that… that THING in my mother's bed is not the person I knew." She stopped the car at a red light and looked at Paul. "Am I a bad person for thinking that?" "Jesus fuck, no Becks!" Paul responded, taken aback for a moment by the severity of the question. "She's been sick for what now… three years? And you've been there for her every step of the way.

You're the strongest woman I know. I'll be damned if I let you feel bad for thinking about YOURSELF for once. You have nothing to blame yourself for! Do you understand that?" Paul put special emphasis on the last sentence, making sure it registered with Rebecca. She smiled, her eyes drifting off into the distance. "Thank you," she said, more to herself than towards him. She wanted to tell him how much she appreciated him as a friend. How much this little conversation helped ease her day. How much it meant to hear these words. "You know, for a pale, small-dicked Irish potatofucker you're not so bad!" They both laughed. The light turned green. Rebecca accelerated the car.

CHAPTER II

Theresa Garmond sat in a cozy chair in what must have been the biggest office she had ever seen. Even compared to her late husband's old workstation, which had been rivaled in size only by his ego, this one was huge. And it was so clean and empty. The center of the room was an old expensive desk made out of dark wood. The obligatory fake monitor and two white chairs, one so new it was clear that whoever owned it didn't spend much of his working day sitting in it, framed the desk in a way that it felt strangely out of place. Behind the desk, one wall of the office was completely dedicated to a huge window that showed the skyline of the city. Theresa was on the upper floors of the Sirona Corp HQ building, so she had a pleasant view while she waited. She would have welcomed some music though. All she could hear was the silent humming of the oxygen bottle standing next to her and the "tick-tock" of the clock hanging on the wall. Both reminded her of how she was slowly but steadily running out of time. Absentmindedly, she hummed an old tune to drown out the clock and the oxygen bottle, only to start coughing almost immediately. "Well, I guess I can't even do that anymore!" she muttered angrily.

Just as Theresa was about to check her watch again, the door to the office opened and a young doctor with blond hair and white teeth bared in a bright smile stormed into the room. He crossed the distance towards her with a couple of energetic strides. "Hello Mrs. Garmond!" he greeted her with a voice equally enthusiastic to his stride. "I hope I haven't kept you waiting for too long." He reached out towards her and shook her hand. "Oh please, stay seated!" Theresa showed no signs of getting up in the first place. One of the few perks of being rich and old: she could be rude and no one dared to call her on her shit. The young doctor sat down in the chair behind the desk and waited a second to make sure he had Theresa's full attention. She knew a salesman when she saw one and he was about to deliver a well-remembered, often practiced and polished sales pitch. "I think we already spoke on the phone, but just in case, my name is Dr. Curtis Locke. I am the head of the Neuro-Transfer Department here at Sirona Corp," Theresa obviously knew who he was. Everyone knew. He was basically the poster child for Sirona's TransLife campaign. Apparently he was also in love with the sound of his voice. "So you are thinking about becoming the newest participant in our TransLife program, isn't that right?" he paused for Theresa to acknowledge his rhetorical question. Theresa wasn't too thrilled to be playing word-games with him, but nodded anyways. "Great! Our Finance Department has already spoken to your lawyers and financial people, and I'm excited to tell you that everything checks out. Both the Transfer as well as the maintenance costs for the Host are covered, so we can leave all the boring stuff behind us!" If she hadn't met slick, money-hungry assholes before, Theresa would have been amazed by the ease with which Locke referred to half a billion dollars. Opting to ignore her growing dislike of Locke, again she chose to listen, taking delight in the growing irritation her passive behavior caused the good doctor. "Have you been briefed on how the process of the Transfer is handled?" He actually waited for her to answer this time. Theresa straightened up in her chair, making it look much more exhausting than it actually was. Unfortunately, she realized that she didn't have to "act" much anymore. With some effort, she managed to look Locke straight in the eye. "I choose from your Hosts on display, you put my consciousness into the brain of the Host, and I walk out here a young woman again. It's not rocket science! So let me stop your prepared speech, which undoubtedly contains loads of big scientific terms that are supposed to impress or confuse me," she said in the cool and calm voice she had used so often in board meetings. "I have more specific questions and I expect you to answer them pointedly and correctly." Theresa took delight in the fraction of a second she was able to pierce the doctor's smiling facade and got a glimpse of his true feelings. Oh, he didn't like her one bit! Still smiling his fake smile, Locke leaned back in his chair and casually crossed his legs. "Sure thing Mrs. Garmond. Ask away!" She could see in his eyes how annoyed he was. Her body might be falling apart, her mind however was still as sharp as ever. And she still loved to toy with people who were eager to get their hands on her money. "So your Hosts were people before, right?" "Yes, that is correct!" "Won't it be crowded in their brains with me in there as well?" Theresa purposely used simple words, trying to bait Locke into feeling cocky and arrogant, ready to shoot him down again if necessary. To his credit the doctor didn't fall for it and started to explain in equally simple words. "No that won't be the case. You see, each of our Hosts has been… for lack of a better term, 'formatted'. When we first acquire the assets, we wipe the hard drives – in this case their brains – and install both our hard- and software." He paused for a second, giving her the chance to interrupt him. "98.2 percent of our assets accept the introduced components without any side effects… given the continuous administration of the provided maintenance substances. For the convenience of our customers, we install the system several months before we add the Host to our portfolio in order to guarantee a smooth Transfer experience." He smiled at her again – his rancid fake smile. "So if you wipe them months ahead of schedule, what do you do with them in the meantime?" Theresa refused to take her gaze off Locke. "Without a consciousness, they need to run a basic operating system that keeps the body functions running. You could compare it to a coma of sorts." "If they're in a coma, won't they have muscle atrophy once I take over?" Theresa continued to poke. Locke raised his eyebrows in surprise. "You are very well informed, Mrs. Garmond. That would be the case if Sirona Corp's first and foremost goal wasn't the client's convenience. Each day, the passive Hosts run what we call an MATP – a Motor Animation Test Program – which basically has them moving for a couple of hours, avoiding muscle atrophy. Several days ahead of the Transfer, we even switch them back from fluid nutrition to 'real' nutrition in order to get the digestive system running again. All that so you, the client, have the most pleasant TransLife experience possible." Locke paused for dramatic effect. "All we ask of you is to stay in our care for 24 hours after the Transfer, just in case." He flashed his phony grandson smile again. "Just in case of what?" Locke took a deep breath, struggling to keep his facade from breaking. "Sometimes there are small… hiccups with Transfers. Your conscience might not map correctly to the Host's brain, for example confusing left and right or not having access to parts of the speech center, etc. In those cases, we need to update the system with a patch to fix those issues. But rest assured, complications like that are few and far between." Theresa arched an eyebrow at him. "Under five percent of all Transfer patients suffer from those minor complications," the doctor answered Theresa's unasked question. Both of them sat there eyeing each other for a moment. Theresa cleared her throat. "What happens to this body once the Transfer is complete?" "Your previous body's brain will be as empty as the Host's brain pre-Transfer. Without any sort of basic input, it will shut down and die. What you do with it is up to you. In most cases, we take care of the… disposal, as our clients are too busy with their new vessels to care about the old ones they left behind. But we had cases in which the client asked for the body to hold a funeral or display it somewhere." Locke looked at her to see if his tasteless taxidermy joke had any impact on her. It didn't. "To be honest, we don't care what you do with it. If we should take care of it for you, just let us know before the Transfer so we can organize the disposal," he finished. His smile was getting old and he visibly struggled to maintain it. "Have you had a look at our portfolio yet?" he asked, eager to move on. "Yes. I will go with Host #23145," Theresa answered, matter of fact.

Doctor Locke put on his glasses, which would allow him to access the database. Unlike most of the staff, he made it a point to remove his glasses whenever he didn't need them. He liked to think it gave people the impression that he cared about what they had to say. Reality couldn't be further from the truth though. Every second he wasted with this old bird was time he couldn't spend with his research. He entered the Host ID she had given him. "I'm afraid I can't offer you #23145!" He already knew before she said anything, that the old bitch wouldn't settle for a simple no. "And why is that?" Theresa asked pointedly. Locke silenced his internal parade of excessive curses and swear words and smiled his trusted "I'm your friend" smile, which seemed to lack any impact on the Garmond bitch. "You see, Host #23145 lived too close to your own residence. We make it a point that our clients only have access to Hosts that used to live at least two hundred miles from the client," The old woman just looked at him, pointing her beaklike nose at him, like a falcon watching its prey. Locke cleared his throat giving himself time to suppress the hot impulse of rage. "During your TransLife, it will happen once or twice that people recognize your Host and, without knowing it, engage with you as if you were still the Host. This is inconvenient and unpleasant, in some cases even dangerous to our clients since, as you know, our Hosts haven't been the most… balanced individuals in their prior life," Not to think of the glitches it would cause with the system, but the old hag didn't need to know anything about that. "These instances would be much more frequent if the Host and the client shared a common residence. So, you will understand if we can't…" "Yeah, I don't care," she cut him off. "As you might be able to attest to by now, I don't care about inconveniences, and I can take care of myself. Have you seen those eyes? I haven't seen pretty green eyes like that on any other Host in your portfolio. I want her! Period!" Locke's smile had finally collapsed. The audacity of that old bitch was more than he could take. "I'm afraid we're at an impasse then." He dropped all pretense of politeness. The old woman started to grin. A feral, almost predatory grin. It disgusted Locke. "An impasse a sizeable and anonymous donation to your private research effort might solve?" she asked, not even trying to hide the bribe. The balls on that bitch! Locke's mind was racing. Could he hide the virtual paper trail well enough so that his superiors wouldn't find it? Was it worth the hassle? Garmond mistook his silence for hesitation. "Ten million." She put a price tag on the bribe. "Twenty!" Locke smiled again, but this time it wasn't his fake grandson smile. It was his true smile. The smile of a reckless man who didn't give two fucks about what happened to that old bird in her new Host.

CHAPTER III

Rebecca and Paul had spent the majority of the afternoon on patrol. It was a calm day. Rebecca could appreciate that, since she still had a headache despite the aspirin she took earlier. It wasn't agonizing, but it was strong enough to let her know it was there and made it hard to focus. She appreciated that Paul took over the heavy lifting – and more importantly the paperwork – as they busted a couple of mind-jackers who had been dealing illegal memories. These vermin tried to cash in on the common folk's desire to experience the same "Memory Making" as rich people did. However, they often – if not always – failed to deliver the same quality, leaving their "clients" in various degrees of mental disarray. Rebecca couldn't help but be bitter about it. She was selling her memories for what felt like pocket money, while a simple "Memory Making" session cost the loaded clients of Sirona Corp anything between two and ten thousand dollars. She didn't even want to think about TransLife. Rebecca was all too aware of the fact that her mother was slowly wasting away in bed vomiting shit, while air-headed bimbos and trophy wives went on to live forever, exchanging their aging body for one of a fresh twenty-year-old as soon as their tits started to sag. Rebecca felt sick to her stomach. She hated the system. But she hated even more that she was part of it, not only because she sold her memories, no but simply by being a cop. After the collapse of the world market fifty years ago, pretty much every major authority – government, civil services, armies, police, firemen etc. – was privately owned. Sirona had already bought and expanded several services all across the States, and people had welcomed them with open arms, even before they owned the media. Around the market crash, everything spiraled into chaos, and Sirona offered the means to reclaim order. The first and so far only time the public took critical note of Sirona's actions was when the government passed the SSA – the Suicide Survivor Agreement – which had survivors of an attempted suicide relinquish all personal and human rights under the care of Sirona Corp, in order to be transformed into Hosts for their TransLife program. But by that time, most members of the government were either part of "TransLife" already or maintaining high-level executive positions at Sirona. There was a public outrage, an online shitstorm, various other governments condemned the SSA – but like with everything else, given enough time, it blew over and the public moved on. And now, whoever attempted suicide and managed to survive anyway, was arrested by cops like Rebecca and Paul and carried off by Sirona representatives, who picked them up right at the precinct. The lucky ones were released a couple of days later, either because they weren't medically cleared or did not pass the "visual standard" TransLife offered their clients. A lot of people were fed up with how things worked, but what can you do if pretty much every decision maker in any kind of authority had ties to the company? So common folk like Rebecca had learned to settle with the current status quo. On days like this however, Rebecca could barely tolerate the injustice of the whole situation. "Are you listening?" Paul dragged her out of her own head and back into reality. "Sorry, what?" She shook her head to clear the cobwebs. "Central Office just called. They need another unit at 32nd Filmore Avenue. Two attempted suicides." Rebecca switched on the siren and turned the car around. Great! Two attempted suicides. The whipped cream on the cherry sundae that was her day!

They arrived at the crime scene a couple of minutes later. A police car and an ambulance already parked in front of the building. Rebecca went to the policeman who had just exited the office. "Hey Johnson. What's up?" The officer nodded as a way of greeting. "We don't really know yet. Either double suicide or murder/suicide. Two victims. One already kicked the bucket. The poor girl was rescued by the EMTs. They say her brain is fried, but she's on life support." "Ah c'mon! You need us to babysit for a potato?" Paul cried out in dismay. "You know the deal guys. The assholes at Sirona can only pick 'em potatoes at the precinct. I need one of you to ride along with the ambulance and deal with the paperwork. I mean, me or Dickson would do it, but we're still waiting for CSI to sweep the place." Johnson added a toneless "Sorry." "Okay then. Meet me at the precinct Becks. I'm going on potato watch!" Paul sighed. "How very Irish of you." She turned to leave for the car when the EMTs brought out the surviving victim. It was her neighbor Diana, the shrink. "Pendejo!" Paul looked at her. "You know her?" "Yeah, she's my neighbor. I just saw her this morning…" Rebecca watched the EMTs load her body into the ambulance. "You know what?" Rebecca walked towards the ambulance, still trying to make sense of the situation. "You did enough paperwork for today already Paul. I'll take this one!" She climbed into the back. "Are you sure?" Paul looked at her concerned. Rebecca nodded, unable to pull her eyes off the lifeless body of Diana, and closed the ambulance doors. They were barely moving when she started to question the EMT riding in the back with her. "So what do you think happened?" Without looking up from the instruments that kept Diana alive, the EMT pointed at the bandages on her wrists. "Tried to off herself by cutting her wrists. Would have worked too if she'd completely sliced the artery, or if we'd been a couple of minutes late to the party. Her brain is already a sponge. We'll see if there's enough non-deteriorated tissue for the Sirona guys to do their thing or if she'll stay a potato." "Her name is Diana!" Rebecca said sharply. The EMT looked at her. "You know her?" Rebecca nodded. "She's my neighbor." "Well…" The EMT awkwardly scratched his head. "My condolences?" "What about the other guy?" Rebecca's mind was racing, trying to remember if she had ever seen a guy with Diana. "Yeah that was weird!" the EMT turned towards his instruments again. "The officers in charge think it was a suicide as well. But something isn't right." "What do you mean?" "I spent half a year with CSI for training. Came across something similar while working a case. The angles of the slices were wrong. Back then, it was someone who tried to stage a murder as suicide. Nearly got away with it too!" The EMT chuckled. "Now he's playing Host for some rich bloke from Boston." "Well if there's a possible murder investigation, Sirona can't have her yet." Rebecca stated matter of fact. The EMT looked at her and gave her a sad smile. "Yeah, but you and I both know that this is up to the officers who first responded to the case. And Johnson hates the arrogant fucks over at Homicide. So fat chance!" He adjusted some values on his instruments. "Who's gonna pay for her life support anyway? On the off chance that she actually has insurance, they'll weasel out of their responsibilities as soon as they hear the word 'suicide'". The EMT's notion was grounded in reality, as Johnson had already ruled the case a double suicide and sent the necessary papers to Rebecca's inbox by the time the ambulance reached the precinct. While she completed the necessary forms for the asset transfer, she couldn't shake the feeling that this wasn't right. The thing the EMT said about the weird angle of the cuts… and

Diana hadn't struck her as someone who would attempt suicide. And what about the other suicide, a certain Robert Jenkins? Johnson's report confirmed that he was not part of Diana's client database, and Diana had never mentioned anything about a boyfriend. Well, Rebecca hadn't asked either, but still. Rebecca handed the tablet over to the Sirona representative, who confirmed the receipt of Diana with his thumbprint. She nodded as he said his goodbyes, then went back to her desk, still in thought. It was Paul who pulled her out of her head, yet again. "You should go home!" "Hm?" She just now realized he was leaning against her desk, looking at her with concern. "You had a long day. First the trouble with your mom, then the Sirona fuckers poked around in your brain, out on patrol all day, and now your neighbor has offed herself. Go home for fuck's sake! Have a nice evening. Grab a beer, eat some burritos and fall asleep in front of the TV. But PLEASE, get out of your head for once!" "You have a weird idea of a nice evening." She gave him a sarcastic grin. "But you're right. I should probably head home." Rebecca rubbed her temples. Paul arched an eyebrow at her as she failed to show any attempt of getting up from her desk and pointed towards the exit. "Yes MOM!" she bleated with mock annoyance. Instead of the beer though, Rebecca ended up giving her mom a bath. Her mother was tired though, so the whole ordeal went over faster than when she had reserves to be aware of the undignified process. She would start a futile attempt to fight her daughter, which would drag out the inevitable for hours. Tonight though, she didn't fight, she didn't even cry. She just lay there and let Rebecca wash her, falling asleep almost instantly after her daughter was done. Rebecca was aware of the brutal irony that what was a "good day" for her probably was a horribly agonizing day of pain for her mother, when she was even too exhausted to cling to the last piece of dignity left to her. Rebecca's dinner consisted of half a box of rice crackers and some leftover Chinese takeout from the day before. With all the crazy things today, Rebecca had forgotten to buy groceries on her way home. She did get some TV time though, as she sat in front of her small set on her ratty old couch and washed the remains of the crackers down with some lukewarm bourbon – the ice compartment of her fridge hadn't worked properly in ages. She even fell asleep, like Paul suggested, during some millennial sitcom re-run. Rebecca dreamt of her neighbor Diana. She was standing next to her and was making small talk, when suddenly Diana stopped mid-sentence and said, "It's just not right!" She grabbed Rebecca by the shoulders and looked at her with those big, sad green eyes. "It's just not right!" "It's just not right!" "It's just not right!" Rebecca woke up on her couch with a short yelp. She was covered in sweat and her heart was racing. All she could think of was Diana and her dream. It just didn't feel right!

CHAPTER IV

Theresa was led into a small white room with two shiny metal stretchers and various instruments which connected the two. Her future Host, the young woman with the beautiful green eyes, was clad in a white patient robe and lying on one stretcher. The other one was for Theresa. Locke was already waiting for her. He smiled his fake, rancid smile while he scanned her with his cruel eyes for any signs of fear. Theresa hated this. The patient robe was less than flattering to her old body, and she'd had an especially bad morning trying to catch her breath. Two technicians were helping her into the room, one holding onto her arm, helping her carry her weight, the other one taking care of her trusted and hopefully soon retired oxygen tank. Theresa felt the full weight of her age today, and she absolutely detested the indignity she had to endure. Plus, despite telling herself otherwise, she was scared of the procedure, and she couldn't stand fear. It clouded judgment, it made you look weak. The presence of Doctor Spineless here didn't help either. Quite the contrary, it made her feel even more uneasy. She lay down on the second stretcher, the oxygen tank on the floor next to her as the technicians left the room. She was alone with the prick now. "How are you doing Mrs. Garmond?" he boomed at her with that obnoxious, overly cheery tone he liked to use. Theresa didn't even dignify his question with an answer. He stood next to the stretcher, towering over her. She had to blink, since he forced her to stare directly into the lights on the ceiling. The little bastard was trying to get even after she took his balls away from him in his office. His smile oozed toxicity as he started to restrain her to the stretcher. "What are you doing?" she asked, alarmed. "Relax Mrs. Garmond." Locke smiled at her, his grin bearing similarities to that of a hyena. "Standard protocol." He nodded over to her new Host, and Theresa realized that the young woman's body was also strapped to the stretcher. To Theresa's surprise, Locke didn't try to hurt her or be overly rough while he restrained her. She had thought he would use the little petty power he had over her to his advantage, but he didn't. She relaxed a bit. "How long will it take?" She had to fight to keep the fear out of her voice. Locke walked away from her and out of view, since she couldn't turn her head anymore due to the restraints. He returned with a crown-like device, which he put on her head. "All in all, two hours, maybe three. It depends on how fast we can map your brain and how similar it is to the Host's." He vanished again from her view and came back with a syringe. "But don't worry, you'll be sedated. It will feel instantaneous to you." Locke positioned himself next to her. Theresa was breathing heavily. She was more afraid than she cared to admit. "Are you ready?" Not trusting her voice to hide her fear, she simply nodded, as much as she could with the headgear and the restraints on her head. He pushed the needle into her arm and injected the contents of the syringe into her vein. "Please count backwards from ten for me, Mrs. Garmond." Locke's voice was all business now. "Ten, nine, ..." The last thing Theresa was aware of before she fell asleep was Locke looking at her with a hateful expression. His smile was gone. Theresa's fear spiked one last time before the darkness swallowed her.

When she awoke, Theresa's head was filled with fog. Thinking was tedious and slow. She felt weird. Her body felt weird. Her eyes were overly sensitive to light. Everything was too bright. Locke's silhouette carved itself from the undefined brightness around her as he bent down to loosen her restraints. "Is it done?" Theresa asked, surprised by the sound of her voice which wasn't her own. Her head slowly reassembled the last memories. Locke faced her and shone a small flashlight in her eyes, testing her reflexes. "What is the last thing you remember Theresa?" He spoke quietly, as her ears were also still overly sensitive. Theresa had to think long and hard on it. "I was getting ready for the Transfer this morning." She paused again. "But I have no memory of getting here." She looked at him frightened. "Don't worry. That is perfectly normal. Unfortunately, we can't transfer fresh memories, so you're missing a couple of hours." He smiled at her and beckoned a technician into the room, who was carrying a wheelchair. "You are lucky. Some of our clients end up missing several days." Locke and the technician helped her into the wheelchair, and for the first time she became aware of herself – her old self – lying on the stretcher next to her. It was a truly weird feeling, seeing the body she had inhabited for almost eighty years. Locke realized what she was looking at. "Don't worry Mrs. Garmond. That is just an empty shell now." "She's... I'm still breathing!" Theresa stated with the voice of the young woman, that so clearly wasn't her own. "Yes." Locke nodded. "It takes the body several minutes to realize that the brain is gone." He nodded to the technician. "This is Charlie, one of our best TransLife Technicians. He'll take you to the Post Transfer Station. There are several physical and psychological tests we need you to complete, to see if everything went right." He paused and flashed his fake smile again. "But I'm sure you'll be walking out of here this time tomorrow, a new person!" Theresa's mind wasn't sharp enough yet to come up with a witty retort, so she just let the technician push her out of the room.

The moment the door closed behind the Garmond bitch's Host, Locke dropped his smile. He locked the door and grabbed another syringe he had hidden in his coat earlier today. He injected the old bird on the stretcher with it, and seconds later, she started to blink. He gave her a minute or two to regain consciousness. "Did it not work?" Her voice slurred as the last traces of sedative left her system. "Oh it worked!" Locke grinned at her viciously. "What do you mean?" Theresa slowly started to grasp the situation she was in. She looked around frantically, as much as her restraints allowed her. "Where is the Host? Where is she?" Locke just grinned at her. "Where is my new body you bastard!" "Walking out of here with a copy of your personality in its head!" His tone made the hairs on Theresa's arm stand up "A copy? You screwed me, you son of a bitch!" Locke laughed. "What? I did exactly what you asked me to! I transferred your consciousness into another body." He obviously enjoyed toying with her. "Then why am I still here?" "Are you aware of what happens to a file on a computer hard drive when you relocate it to a different folder? The file is copied over to the new location and is deleted in its old folder." He took pleasure in the growing terror in Theresa's eyes and moved in close to her until his mouth was next to her ear. "There is no magical re-location without getting rid of the old version," he whispered. "You… I have powerful friends! I will have you–" Theresa stuttered, her mind paralyzed by fear as the reality of her situation sunk in. She started to fight against the restraints as much as her weak body allowed it to. "You?" Locke sneered at her. "Your new you is already out there. No one knows the old you still exists." He moved his face even closer, until they were only inches apart. "And now I'm going to delete the old version," Locke hissed, looking her straight in the eye. "If you ask nicely, I might even put you back to sleep before I start!"

Several minutes later, Locke left the room as the technicians carried out the covered-up body of Theresa Garmond. Locke felt content. He hadn't liked the way the old bitch had played him during their meeting, so he decided to get even. It was a stupid risk to take, and he'd thought it over several times. Even when she had walked into the Transfer Room earlier today, he hadn't been quite sure yet if he would go through with it. Locke was very aware of his ego, how it posed a liability to him and his work. When he was young, it had gotten him into loads of trouble. But Locke was also very smart – much more than anyone gave him credit for – so he had learned to balance out his egoistic tendencies with reason. But earlier, when the old bitch refused to show some humility in the presence of his work and didn't show any intimidation in the face of what was in his mind the greatest invention of the last two centuries, she had sealed her fate. Was it petty of him? Yes, surely. But Locke was fine with that, because he knew he could get away with it. Sometimes even men like him needed to embrace their flaws. Not only had he gained personal satisfaction from it, he also got rid of a liability. Normally he didn't do the Transfers himself, but he wanted to make sure to minimize the risk of a technician stumbling over memories of the bribe while wiping the old bird. With old Garmond out of the way, only two people knew of the bribe he had taken, and without knowing it, the other witness had moved herself into a position that would narrow the number down to Locke alone sooner than later.

CHAPTER V

Two months had passed since Diana had attempted suicide. Rebecca's initial unease about the situation had washed over in the face of her day-to-day life. Her mother had bad phases and good phases, but the writing on the wall was clear. It wouldn't take long now. Rebecca opened the door to her mother's room each day, half expecting that she'd stopped breathing overnight. And Rebecca hated herself for that tang of annoyance that crept into her mind each time she found her mother still alive. She had called in every favor under the sun to minimize her working hours to spend more time with her mother, who needed more care now than ever before. Even if that meant that Rebecca could barely pay the rent. Last month, Paul had lent her money so she could take care of the electricity bill, and despite Rebecca fighting him tooth and nail for it, like the stubborn Irish bastard he was, he hadn't taken no for an answer. He was a good friend. He might be even more than a good friend someday... after her mother. And there it was again. The sharp pain of guilt. Rebecca massaged her temples and took a deep breath. She peeked in her mother's bedroom to make sure she was asleep before she left the apartment. She needed groceries. Rebecca went down the road towards the store when she caught a glimpse of something familiar – no, someONE familiar – in her peripheral vision. She looked at the woman on the other side of the street. Rebecca was baffled. It was Diana, getting out of an expensive looking car. She was dressed differently than normal, and she wore her hair different, but it was definitely her. Technically, Rebecca knew that this couldn't be Diana. Even if Diana's body hadn't been taken over by some rich client of Sirona, the EMTs had told her she was brain-dead. But in the heat of the moment Rebecca didn't think clearly and started crossing the street, waving at what she wished to be Diana, craving some sort of normal interaction that didn't revolve around her mother slowly wasting away. The other woman took notice of Rebecca as well and looked at her puzzled. Rebecca's rational mind finally took charge again as she awkwardly stopped mid-wave and felt her cheeks blush. The two looked at each other awkwardly. "I must have gotten you mixed up with someone else…" Rebecca tried to avoid eye contact. "I'm sorry." She turned on her heel and walked back the way she came from, feeling stupid, the other woman's irritated gaze burning a hole in the back of her head.

Theresa was puzzled by the young Latina woman who had so enthusiastically greeted her on the street. She had no memory of meeting her before. What was it that Locke had said? Her Host used to live in this area? Well what do you know, the self-absorbed slimebag actually had told her SOMETHING that was correct. Theresa just wished he had spoken the truth about the rest of the post-Transfer complications as well. It had been two days since she first inhabited her new Host, and she still didn't feel the same. It started with small complications after the Transfer, because of course she had to be among the five percent. So Doctor Locke had come to visit her a couple of hours after her Transfer to administer a patch, which solved the problems with her speech center. During her former life, she had learned three different foreign languages, which after the Transfer she couldn't understand anymore when someone was talking to her. She could read them just fine, but her audio understanding was messed up. The patch however worked, so she at least got something out of yet another unpleasant run-in with Locke. What the patch didn't solve was the headaches she got in the morning after waking up, and the overall feeling that she wasn't using her body herself. It was hard to describe. It felt like she was remote controlling the Host and the world around her was more of a simulation than the real deal. Two days and Theresa was already starting to question her decision. By signing the TransLife Agreement with Sirona Corp, Theresa had committed herself to attending a special Post Transfer Therapy that she had to participate in daily for the first three months of her TransLife. She had been on her way to the shrink when she had a run-in with the young woman on the street. She dreaded going back to that shrink, a horrible human being, named Doctor Henry Thomas. A short, fat, balding man who smelled of junk food, coffee and cheap cologne. Theresa had never liked people who let themselves go. Appearances meant everything. It also didn't help that, apparently, Theresa's Host used to be a shrink as well, and Thomas and her Host had attended a conference together. So, whenever Doctor Thomas looked at Theresa, she felt like he was actually looking at the person that used to be her Host. Add to that the fact that Theresa never liked shrinks anyway – she considered the whole idea of a therapy ridiculous and a scam for money – and she found herself in a daily obligation for the next three months that she did not exactly look forward to. She entered the building of Doctor Thomas' medical practice and called the elevator. Theresa couldn't shake the feeling that she'd forgotten something. She snapped around as she tried to find her oxygen tank, only to remember a second later that she didn't need it anymore. That was the third time she had looked for a phantom oxygen tank today. This whole TransLife business was far more impeding on her daily routine than she had been promised beforehand. Her initial plan was to start attending board meetings again a week after the Transfer, but so far, it didn't seem like that would be possible. She couldn't let those jackals on the board see her weak and confused like that. Theresa was not happy at all. And what was the deal with that Latina? Theresa wasn't an especially racist person all her life, but the woman DID look suspicious. What if her Host had some shady operation going with that person, illegally selling prescription meds? Maybe she felt like Theresa was a threat to her. No… Theresa shook her head. She was being paranoid. Or was she? Suddenly, a sharp pain shot through Theresa's forehead. She doubled over and clutched her head, moaning in pain, struggling to stay on her feet. She closed her eyes as her mind was attacked by brightly flashing images of that woman from the street. But it was not on the street. It was in the hallway of an apartment building Theresa had never seen before. Another image, this time of a room. Of a wall in said room with an ugly painting of a sailboat on it. It didn't make sense. The pain left her head as quickly as it appeared. "What the hell?" Was this yet another side effect of the Transfer? Was that because she had run into the woman on the street? Damn her, why had she talked to Theresa! Another flash of paranoia. Maybe she had done it on purpose… "Goddamn it Theresa, pull yourself together!" Yet again, Theresa regretted her decision to join TransLife. She should have faced death with some dignity. Obviously the process wasn't as smooth as Doctor Locke had made it out to be. If there was one thing Theresa treasured above all else, it was her ability to stay reasonable in almost any situation. But that seemed to be gone now. Theresa felt hot tears flowing down her face. "Oh what the hell…" She hadn't cried in forty years. What was wrong with her?

She did not have control over herself. And Theresa hated nothing more than not being in control!

CHAPTER VI

"Send him in please!" Locke answered the call of his secretary. He didn't look forward to the meeting, but it had to be done. He hated the guys from Asset Containment. They even gave him the creeps. The Asset Containment Unit, or ACU in short, was the TransLife program's safety line. Each member of ACU was a former soldier and a contractor to Sirona. They agreed to basically sell their bodies and combat sharpened instinct to Sirona for "administrational and security issue related activities". To put it bluntly, they did the dirty work for the company. At the beginning, their emotional triggers were wiped from their brains during their five-year service to make them more susceptible to suggestion and less prone to their voice of conscience. Additionally, they underwent a mandatory memory wipe every three months to make sure that there were no longtime leaks of their operations, which often bordered on the illegal. One might ask why anyone would agree to that kind of job. Well, the pay was extraordinarily good, and the minds of retired ACU handlers were reconstructed to the same state they had when they first accepted the job. So from their perspective, the five years went by in an instant, and their accounts boasted an unholy amount of money. However, the suppressed emotional triggers and the frequent wipes had the side effect that an active ACU handler gave off a rather sociopathic vibe that Locke found to be very unsettling, his brain trained by eons of evolution, flagging the handlers as a potential danger. He made it a point to deal as little with them as possible. But this time, he needed to "borrow" one of the ACU handlers for some of his own "operations". The handler entered the room, clad in the ACU's typical non-specific black and dark navy blue uniform that didn't differ much from the usual uniforms worn by generic security services all over the world. He – Locke liked to think of ACU handlers more as an "it" though – walked straight towards Locke's desk and stood in front of it, straight as an arrow, chest out, stomach sucked in and arms crossed behind his back. It probably took him all his restraint to refrain from saluting. The doctor looked at him with irritation. He'd never thought much of the military; a bunch of brutes with an alpha male mentality, whose petty attempts at "conflict solving" over the millennia had only changed in regards to what kind of stick they used to beat each other to death with. Locke sneered at the handler, but was taken aback as he saw him looking straight at Locke with expressionless eyes, waiting to receive orders. "I need you to start surveillance on an asset in the field," Locke addressed the handler. "We believe that there have been consequences which triggered an overreaction in one of our built-in recursive functions." Locke put it as nonspecific as possible. A lot of executive personnel tended to be too specific with the ACU handlers, since they would get wiped anyways. An unnecessary risk in Locke's eyes. He was more than aware of how much they had yet to understand about the human mind to not take the chance to tell the handler about – how had that nosy shrink bitch called it – the "Foreign Effect". "We believe the asset could pose a danger to not only herself, but her surroundings as well. Everything you need to know about the asset is in this file." He punched a key on his keyboard and sent the file to the handler's inbox. Locke waited a minute watching the handler's eyes flicker behind the glasses as he was reading the file. After the handler had finished and his eyes focused back on Locke, the doctor continued: "I want you to send me a surveillance report every twelve hours. But DO NOT engage the asset at any rate. Do you understand that?" "Yes Sir!" The handler did not take his eyes off Locke. "Alright, dismissed!" With an annoyed hand gesture Locke beckoned the handler to leave him. The handler left his office, and Locke felt himself exhale sharply. He wasn't aware that he had held his breath in the presence of the handler. "Goddamn robots!" He turned around in his chair. Looking out of the huge window, his gaze wandering over the skyline of the city. Locke had received word from Doctor Thomas, the Garmond bitch's assigned shrink. Apparently, the old bird was still struggling with adapting to the Host's body. On top of that, she had her first run-in with an acquaintance of the Host's former life, which had sent her subconscious into overdrive. She was experiencing memories that weren't her own. Nothing conclusive of course. It was the subconscious after all. Pictures, associated feelings, etc. Nothing to actually make sense of. If those visions wouldn't drive her mad, the recursive factor that Locke had increased about twice its normal value, specifically for Garmond, would do the job and erase the last witness of Locke's newfound extended wealth. Locke was proud of his work. Not only was he about to tie up the little bribe affair neatly and cleanly, no, administering the patch to mess with the recursive factor and hiding that specific function in the fix for her speech center was tricky and – in Locke's eyes at least – a work of art. It had been a while since Locke had felt satisfaction from his work. He grinned as he browsed through the file he had sent the handler. Such a pretty Host. It would be a shame to let a vessel like that go to waste! Locke took off his glasses and allowed himself to feel content. Soon he would have dealt with this issue and everything could go on as usual!

CHAPTER VII

Theresa was desperate. Two days had passed since she had met the Latina woman on the street. Two days since she started to have those painful flashbacks of places and people she didn't know. Over the span of those two days, the episodes had worsened in both the pain they put her through and the frequency in which they appeared. Theresa hadn't left the house since. Doctor Thomas had tried to reach her several times but she had blocked him on all channels. The worst part about those flashes was that the pain she felt was the only thing she truly recognized as real, as her own. Everything else wasn't. The feeling of detachment and "remote-controlling" her Host had intensified. Theresa wasn't rested when she woke up, because it wasn't her who was sleeping. Food and drinks tasted bland and weird, because it wasn't her tongue that tasted them. And it wasn't her stomach either, so no matter if she ate or not, she stayed hungry. Or was she even hungry? Theresa couldn't tell anymore. The sunlight seemed fake, like from a lightbulb, so she closed the blanks and spent the day in the dark left to her thoughts and fears. Yesterday she let go of the house staff. She couldn't stand their accusing gazes. She felt like she heard them whispering behind her back constantly. Maybe they were conspiring? Maybe they knew her Host in her previous life? The rational part of Theresa's mind knew that she was being paranoid. But the longer it took, the less reasons she found to fight her paranoia. If everything was fake and she was the only one realizing it, didn't that say something? She'd always been more intelligent and quick-minded than other people. What if that son of bitch Locke had screwed her over and she wasn't really transferred? Maybe her mind was trapped in some sort of simulation. Yes… YES, that had to be it. That was why everything felt fake. And everyone was in on the joke except her. They were laughing at her. Making fun of her. Entertaining themselves watching her suffer and try to make sense of things. Theresa cried out as another flash ravaged her brain. Again, that Latina woman in the apartment floor. Again, that wall with the shitty painting of a sailboat. She doubled over, falling to the floor as she clutched her head, squeezing it with both hands in a fruitless attempt to override the pain with a different sensation. Another flash – a new one this time. She saw herself… no her Host. Looking at herself in the mirror – staring down her reflection with those big green eyes. But suddenly, it wasn't her reflection anymore. It was Theresa. Eighty-year-old Theresa, staring back at the young woman from the other side of the mirror. "Find her," the young woman uttered almost tonelessly. "FIND HER!" she screamed again and the flash came to an end. The pain subsided, and Theresa was lying there on the floor, in the dark, sobbing openly. God how she hated crying. Every bone in her body ached. No, not her body. She felt the pain as if it was filtered. As if it was washed out in some weird way. This had to stop. She had lost. Everyone else had won. She'd had a chance to end her life with some dignity, but she'd preferred to make an ass out of herself. And now she was paying for it. Theresa picked herself up off the ground, feeling older than she had ever felt in her old body. She pulled her bathrobe tight around her, hugging herself with her arms. Theresa had always loved this bathrobe. Its silky surface and the smell of many steamy baths. Normally, putting it on calmed Theresa and filled her with joy. The anticipation of a bath – literally letting her hair down for once. She had put the robe on yesterday in a desperate attempt to calm herself. But even the robe felt fake now. The way it brushed against her skin... different. Theresa slowly wandered through the house like a ghost. She went down to the wine cellar to pick up a bottle of her favorite red and up again in the kitchen to pour herself a glass before going to the bathroom. She opened the valves and poured hot water into the tub. A good bath had always done its magic on her. The last resort of her confused mind. She watched the water slowly fill the tub as she added her favorite lemon bath salt. It didn't smell like anything special to her now. The warm, damp air fogged up the inside of the bathroom window as she stopped the hot water pouring into the tub. Absentmindedly she stared into the tub as she swirled her fingers through the hot, rising water. She loosened her beloved bathrobe and climbed into the tub. The heat bit her skin as she sat down and let it engulf her almost completely. As the foam of the bath salts tickled her chin, Theresa closed her eyes – those green eyes she had wanted so badly – and submerged her head for a second before she came back up again and brushed her hair out of her face. She settled down and breathed in the aromatic fumes of the bath. Again: bland and filtered. Like a faint memory of what a bath was supposed to smell like. Theresa reached for the glass of wine she had put on the small side table next to the tub. She sipped on it, and her gaze wandered towards the ceiling of the elegantly furnished bathroom. She swirled the sip around in her mouth. Her favorite wine. It tasted like chalky water. Her free hand resting on her thigh, Theresa chuckled – a sad, cynical chuckle – as she let her fingers run over her smooth young skin. The outer shell of her masquerade. An old woman pretending to be a twenty-year-old girl. She must have been stupid to think this could work! "Who would have thought it would come to this." Theresa awkwardly wrapped her fingers around the wineglass and squeezed them until it shattered. She cut herself as it disintegrated in her palm, but again, the pain felt far away, not real. With childlike amazement, she watched as the red wine mixed itself with her blood and ran down her forearm. She got hold of a big and sharp shard and turned it, the light reflecting in its surface as well as the wet blood stains on it, and chuckled again. In eighty years on this earth, Theresa had never thought she'd find herself in this situation. She had never backed down before, but with every passing second, quitting felt more and more like the right thing to do. Tears started to form in those goddamned green eyes, and once more she was crying. Quietly sobbing, her voice breaking, she started to hum the melody of "What a Difference a Day Makes" as she slowly led the shard towards her wrist. She lightly pressed the glass against her skin and stopped. "What the hell are you doing Theresa?" she spoke out loudly. Suddenly shocked at her own behavior, she threw the shard away as far as she could. Theresa buried her face in her hands. Was she going insane? Was this what madness felt like? She screamed out again as another flash washed over her. The apartment hall, the Latina woman, the painting and the green eyes in the mirror. "Find her! FIND HER!" Theresa gasped as the pain let off. For a second, she just lay there in the bathtub, looking at the ceiling. Those images burned in her head. Somehow, they felt different from all the other flashes Theresa experienced. Like they had a purpose. The hallway and the woman. The painting in the office. The instructions in front of the mirror. It almost felt deliberate. She had to find that hallway. She had to find that woman. Maybe it would stop these goddamn flashes. But what if it didn't? Theresa chuckled sadly. What other options were there? Slowly go insane? Frightened, Theresa looked at the glass shard lying on the floor on the other end of the bathroom. No. She never backed down. She would not wait until her mind would fail her completely. She would not wait until that shard became the only way out that made sense. "Find her," she muttered as she slowly climbed out of the bathtub, still shaking.

CHAPTER VIII

"Let me help, for fuck's sake Rebecca!" Paul shouted at her. "I don't want you to help me AGAIN!" Rebecca screamed back at him with the first signs of tears in her eyes. "What kind of daughter am I if I can't handle this by myself?" She let herself fall down on her trusted ratty couch, burying her face in her hands, muttering something self-loathing in Spanish. If she was about to cry, she didn't want Paul to see it. That goddamned ER bill… Rebecca's mother had had an emergency a couple of days ago. Rebecca had come back from buying groceries when she found her mother choking. She had thrown up in her sleep. If Rebecca had been a minute late, her mother would have suffocated. As the EMTs carried her mother to the hospital and Rebecca realized that this would mean another hospital bill, she found herself thinking about why she couldn't have been late. And of course, as always, this was followed by an immense wave of guilt and self-loathing as she caught up with her train of thought. Her mother was admitted and now was breathing through a respirator in the intensive care ward. Intensive care meant intensive bills, and so Rebecca stared at several hundred dollars of medical bills for each day her mother lived on. Since her neighbors had told the officials that she left her mother alone while she was buying groceries, she also wasn't allowed to take her back home. It wasn't like the doctors could do anything for her mother. They just prolonged the inevitable and milked Rebecca for every cent she had left. Paul had called several times before, but Rebecca just passed him straight to voicemail. She didn't want to deal with him. After he couldn't reach her for a whole day, he came by and found her wallowing in self-pity and bourbon. So she had to tell him, and OF COURSE, he offered to help her pay the bills. She knew he would. That was part of why she didn't want to talk to him. She needed to pay those bills herself. Atone for her fucking selfishness. "Stop punishing yourself Becks!" Paul ripped her out of her thoughts. His voice suddenly became quiet. "I can't watch you punish yourself any longer for things you have no control over." He sat down next to her, his gaze emptily wandering over the floor. "All you do is care for your mom. Fuck, you even crippled your head for her, letting those Sirona fucks weasel around in your mind! Please Becks, I'm begging you! If I ever meant anything to you, let me help you!" He fought back tears. Rebecca looked at him, confused. There was an awkward silence between them. Paul was being overly intimate again. Yes, they were friends, and yes, he cared a bit more about her than normal friends do, but this… this felt weird. "Where the hell did that come from? Meant anything to me? Dude, we're friends, but… what?" Paul looked at her in shock, trying to form words. Something shifted behind his eyes, and his shoulders slumped as he realized the situation. "Becks, we were dating for almost a year! What are YOU talking about?" "What?" "Hell, I even took you to Paris for a weekend!" He got up from the couch and looked at her furiously. Nothing. Rebecca had no memory of a thing like this. The emptiness in Paul's eyes turned to a silent plea. And once he realized what had happened, something ugly reared inside him. "You sold them! You gave away our relationship to those Sirona fuckers!" Paul started to chuckle bitterly. "Well I hope it was a fucking grade A memory!" he spat at her, his voice breaking and tears streaking down his face, his expression almost feral. Paul's body went limp as he tried to collect himself. "I always had the suspicion. But I never could bring myself to ask." Again the bitter chuckle and a long pause. "Fuck you Rebecca." He pulled his wallet out of his back pocket, opened it and threw a crumpled photograph towards Rebecca. Without another word, he left her apartment, smashing the door shut behind him. Rebecca, confused and terrified by what had just happened, picked up the photograph and turned it around. It was her and Paul. They both looked younger. In the background, she could see the Arc de Triomphe... so they'd been to Paris...? Obviously she couldn't remember what memories she'd given up, but she wouldn't put it past herself to sell a memory of Paul's and her relationship right after they broke up. When it hurt the most. When you didn't think rationally. When you're hurt and eager to get even. She knew that she hadn't handled heartache all too well in the past. It all made sense now. Paul's loyalty and kindness despite her never doing much to deserve that kind of friendship. She had kept him on a leash without knowing it. Rebecca collapsed on the couch under the weight of her own guilt, sobbing, not holding anything back. She cried until she couldn't cry any more. Until her body ached from the convulsions. Until her eyes were an angry red from all the tears and her eyeballs burned against the inside of her eyelids. Eventually she fell asleep. She awoke several hours later. It was the middle of the night and someone was banging on her door. Still dazed and in the early stages of a hangover, she stumbled to her apartment door. She opened it and stared into the green eyes of Diana. "I think we need to talk.".

CHAPTER IX

Theresa didn't have to look long for the woman. After her breakdown in the bathtub, she found new resolve in focusing on a goal: finding the woman in her visions. And at least for now, it helped. Theresa had driven to the neighborhood where she had run into the woman for the first time and started checking all the apartment complexes around. She knew what the corridors in the building she was searching for looked like from the flashes. That was a place to start from. Theresa was lucky. The corridors in the third apartment building she entered did not only match her visions, entering the building also triggered another painful episode. After it passed, Theresa focused her mind on the positive. She was in the right building. She was getting closer. She could do something about her situation. The woman in her visions obviously was Latina, so Theresa checked the residents for typical last names. Theresa was lucky again. Only four tenants of the building had Latin-American last names. The first door Theresa knocked on – ignoring the fact that it was almost 3am – belonged to an "E. Guerrero", who turned out to be a fat dude in his forties with a pissy attitude and a temper.

Theresa couldn't afford to get sidetracked. She didn't know how long she could hold herself together before she lost her mind again. The minute Mr. Guerrero started shouting at her, Theresa just turned around and left for the next door. Angry insults flung her way in a thick accent followed her up the stairs, where her knocking on the door of "M. Sanchez" resulted in absolutely no reaction at all. Either Sanchez wasn't home, or he didn't want to open the door in the middle of the night. Desperately, Theresa knocked on the third door on the same floor. She didn't want to wait until the second door's inhabitant showed up. God only knew if she would be able to keep it together for that long, or if she ended up throwing herself off the building. She couldn't trust her mind anymore. When Rebecca Gonzalez finally opened the door, Theresa almost hugged her. A huge stone fell off her chest. She had found her, now she needed to get her to listen. Theresa noticed that the other woman was wearing a crumpled and stained police uniform, and a flash of paranoia gripped her. She was part of the system. Everyone knew that Sirona worked with the local authorities. Come to think of it, wasn't she followed on her way here? Theresa could have sworn that a gray sedan had been in view all the way from her house, always trying to stay out of sight. No! Theresa shook her head. Her focus was cracking up again. She forced her mind to quiet down. "We need to talk," she addressed the other woman. "I know you know me." The policewoman mustered her from head to toe. She looked tired and worn out, deep shadows under her swollen red eyes. Well look who's talking, Theresa thought to herself, keenly aware of how she… or her Host must look by now. "I know who you used to be," the other woman finally said with a matter-of-fact, no bullshit voice, which she had undoubtedly picked up as a cop. "Yes. I am a TransLife participant. But something is not right. I keep remembering your face, among other things." Theresa was eager to get out of the open hallway. She hastily looked to her left and right, her paranoia acting up again. "Can I come in?"

Rebecca hesitated. Diana... or what used to be Diana looked at her with a frantic expression. Apparently the other woman was highly anxious about staying out in the corridor. Rebecca beckoned her to come in and closed the door behind her, suddenly very aware of the Glock she had stored in the kitchen counter, for emergencies. "You wanted to talk? Talk." Rebecca eyed the other woman, who had sat down on her couch, obviously relieved to be out of the hallway. "My name was... is Theresa Garmond. I was transferred into this body a couple of days ago. But ever since that, everything feels wrong." She looked at Rebecca, who had positioned herself near the kitchen counter, still tensed up and ready to go for her hidden gun. "I can feel my mind falling apart... and I keep having visions of you and... her." Theresa pointed at herself. It took Rebecca a while to understand that the other woman meant Diana. "Visions of me?" Theresa nodded, looking like she was about to break out in tears. "How do you know her?" Again, she pointed at herself. "She used to be my neighbor. She tried to kill herself a couple of months ago. I guess that's how she ended up for sale." Rebecca put all the disdain she could muster into the last two words. It was lost on Theresa however, who looked like a squirrel on drugs, trying desperately to put the puzzle pieces together. "Was there anything weird about her suicide attempt?" "Why? What are you thinking?" Rebecca was suddenly curious. She allowed herself to lower her guard a bit. "You see, the visions I'm having are always the same. You in the corridor of this apartment building, a painting of a sailboat in a room, followed by me... her, telling me to 'find her'." She paused for a moment. "It feels oddly deliberate don't you think? Almost like a map." Rebecca looked at her, not entirely sure she understood. "It almost feels like my Host..." "Diana," Rebecca interrupted pointedly. "Diana... wanted me to find you."

Theresa looked at the other woman, hoping against hope she would believe her. Both women intently stared at each other for a long moment. "Okay," Rebecca finally broke the silence. She pulled the Glock out of the kitchen board and put it pointedly on the couch table as she sat down across from Theresa. "I'm not saying I believe you, but there is enough weird shit in your story that adds up." Rebecca tried to act as much in control of the situation as possible. Take control of the situation. Handle it! Her mother's mantra. "Start from the beginning. Tell me everything. Every detail."

Locke was ripped out of the depths of sleep by his cell phone going off in the middle of the night. He struggled to focus as he tried to decipher the caller's identity. It was the ACU handler he had put on the Garmond bitch. What the hell? His next report wasn't due until noon. "This better be worth my time!" Locke said as he picked up the call. "The asset has established contact with a former acquaintance of the Host," the handler's monotone voice echoed in Locke's ear. "So?" "She purposefully and directly looked for her and found her. Given her previous behavior, this might pose a problem," the handler wasn't fazed by Locke's bored undertone. Locke's mind tried to escape the last ties of sleep as he pieced one and two together. He knew that the increased recursive factor had already shown devastating effects on Garmond, since she didn't attend her therapy any longer. According to the ACU handler, she hadn't left the house for days either and fired the entire staff of her mansion. Another symptom of growing paranoia. Normally, she should have tried to off herself by now. The old bird was as stubborn as ever. Locke's thoughts were slow and sluggish as he tried to form coherent conclusions. "What's the name of the Host's acquaintance?" "Officer Rebecca Gonzalez, her neighbor. Apparently she works for the local police force. Mostly patrol duty." Gonzalez... Locke tried to remember where he had read that name before. Ah yes, of course! She was the cop who had handled the asset acquisition. Locke didn't like that. Cops were nosey, and the Garmond case especially was not the kind of business Locke wanted anyone to be nosey about. It was time to pull the plug on this thing. "Contain the asset and bring Gonzalez to me. I want to talk to her." He would offer Gonzalez a bribe and, if necessary… clean up the situation. If push came to shove, he could spin it accordingly afterwards to make it look like the asset went nuts and her former neighbor, unfortunately, fell victim to the situation. The more he thought about it Locke preferred the second situation. It was cleaner and more… permanent. It would be bad PR for TransLife, but nothing compared to the shitstorm a leak of the shrink's data would mean for Sirona. "Scratch that!" Locke revised his order. "Contain the asset and dispose of the witness. I want this to be handled as low-profile as possible. Understood?" "Understood." The handler hung up.

CHAPTER X

Theresa told Rebecca every detail she remembered about the TransLife process and Locke. She also told her about the side effects and her recent breakdown. Rebecca for her part talked about Diana and how her suicide came out of the blue. How it felt weird to Rebecca to begin with. With every passing minute, the Glock on the table became more irrelevant as she dove deep into the whole TransLife situation. Rebecca used her police ID to access the casefiles online. For the first time since Diana's suicide attempt, she looked at the details, especially on the guy who died alongside her, Robert Jenkins. As Rebecca already knew, he was not a patient of Diana's, so what was he doing in her practice? She went through Jenkins' file. "Hm weird…" "What?" Theresa's gaze was glued to Rebecca's face. "Jenkins has two priors for mindjacking. Our mysterious pseudo boyfriend was a biohacker." Rebecca averted her eyes from the tablet and let her stare go blank for a second. "You said the visions you experience feel almost like they had a purpose?" Theresa nodded repeatedly. Rebecca kept thinking. "I remember there being a mindjacking case a couple of years back. The hacker hijacked the victim's brains and planted a behavior routine in their subconscious. The victims would mail all their sensitive data back to the hacker while sleepwalking, without ever remembering that they did." Rebecca paused for a second. "The reason it took us forever to figure out was that even the anti-mindjacking devices Sirona supplies us with have no access to the subconscious. If it is possible to hide whole behavior patterns in there, it should be possible for a biohacker to plant a couple of visual cues as well." Theresa's eyes went wide. Rebecca shook her head. "No… something's off. The behavior in that case was triggered by a specific phrase, planted in an email the hacker sent the victims. I remember one of the Sirona eggheads specifically stressing that it wouldn't have worked otherwise." Theresa jumped up. "But that's how it worked!" Rebecca looked at her confused. "I didn't have any visions until I ran into you on the street. Seeing you must have been the trigger!" "So what? You're telling me that Diana had a biohacker implant a series of visual cues in her subconscious that would lead whoever would take her on as a Host to me?" Rebecca wasn't really sure she was believing what she was saying. Theresa nodded excitedly. "But why would she do that?" Theresa's shoulders slumped as the realization hit her that they still weren't any wiser.

Suddenly someone knocked on the door. Both women froze. Who was that? Rebecca looked at her watch. It is barely past 6 AM. She reached for her Glock and switched the safety off, holding the gun behind her back as she slowly approached the apartment door. "Who is it?" She raised her voice so that whoever was outside could hear her. "Miss Gonzalez, please open the door! You are in acute danger!" a deep, brutish voice boomed from the other side. "WHO. IS. IT?" Rebecca's voice took on a more demanding tone. "Sirona Asset Containment Unit. Listen lady, the Host you are currently sheltering poses a significant threat to herself as well as everyone around her.

Please let me in!" Rebecca looked at Theresa, who shook her head slowly, silently voicing "Do NOT open the door!" The second it took Rebecca to think what she should do next was enough for the ACU handler to act. There was a loud noise as the door lock shattered against the frame. Taken by surprise, Rebecca had the air knocked out of her as the door slammed into her. She fell to the ground, losing her grip on the gun. The handler – a big, muscular jarhead clad in indistinct black clothes – stepped into the apartment, gun in hand. He kicked the Glock out of Rebecca's reach as he pointed his gun alternately towards Rebecca or Theresa. Rebecca's eyes widened as she realized the gun was equipped with a silencer. She suddenly knew why the ACU handler was here. They were truly in deep shit. He gripped Rebecca by her hair and pushed her into the room next to Theresa before closing the door behind him. Since he had broken the lock when he kicked it open, all the handler could do was close it over. "This could have gone a lot more pleasantly if you would have complied." His free hand went to his back pocket and produced some sort of headgear that looked oddly familiar to the device Rebecca knew from her "Memory Making" sessions. Slowly, he approached Theresa, who backed away into a corner, gripped by terror. Pleadingly, she looked towards Rebecca, but with the gun fixed on her there was nothing the police woman could do. The handler put the device on Theresa's head. She looked at Rebecca, her green eyes filled with the sudden realization that this was it. This was as far as she would go. Theresa's sobs stopped and she closed her eyes. For one last instance, she felt the composure and calm she used to have. At least she would die as herself. The handler pressed a switch on the headgear. Theresa's body went limp and fell to the floor. Her eyes blankly stared into the room. "What the fuck did you just do?" Rebecca uttered in pure terror. "She's not dead. My employer would never waste a quality Host," the handler removed the headgear from Theresa and put it back into his pocket. "I merely performed an emergency reset and put the basic operating system back in place." Rebecca felt a chill run down her spine as the handler matter-of-factly told her what he just did. "That way she stays alive until the EMTs find her later, surviving yet another suicide attempt." Rebecca felt the need to physically repel even further from the brutish figure in her living room. "Unfortunately, a former acquaintance of the Host was killed by the asset beforehand." The handler tightened the grip on his pistol and aimed it directly at Rebecca's head Just as the handler was ready to pull the trigger, the apartment door opened. "Becks are you okay, your door is brok–" Paul was dressed in his uniform – probably on his way to work. He saw the lifeless woman on the floor and the brutish guy with the gun trained on Rebecca. It took him a moment to react as he reached for his own gun. The handler whirled around and shot. Paul hugged the floor and evaded the projectile. As he was trying to fire back, the handler had already crossed the room and mercilessly buried his boot in Paul's face, which exploded in a gush of blood, saliva and teeth. With the gun no longer trained on her, Rebecca dove for her Glock, which was still lying on the floor. Just as the handler was about to shoot Paul, who desperately clutched the bloodied mess that used to be his face, Rebecca came back up, Glock in hand, and without hesitation pulled the trigger. The sound of gunshots echoed from the walls of her living room as she shot twice. The first shot missed the target, but the second shot buried itself in the handler's shoulder. Alarmed by the gunshots, several people came running out of their apartments and saw the handler standing in the broken door of Rebecca's apartment. He looked around calmly, apparently unphased by the bullet in his shoulder, put away his pistol and left. For a minute Rebecca stood frozen with the Glock in her hand before Paul's moans snapped her out of it. She crossed the room and kneeled next to him. "Let me see," she said with a calm voice. She half guided, half pulled Paul's hands away from his face. The handler's boot had done a number on Paul. His nose was definitely broken, his lips were swollen and cut open, and he was missing his upper front teeth. Also, his left eye had taken on a deep purple color and was slowly closing up. The other eye looked up at her, the unspoken question of "How bad is it?" lingering in its gaze. "Shit Paul, you've always been ugly, so I don't really see a difference," Rebecca tried to joke and nearly choked on her words. Paul chuckled. "Affhole," he mumbled. Rebecca could hear police sirens in the distance and looked at the lifeless body of Theresa. They were fucked. Sirona would find a way to pin this on her, or worse, on Paul. They had to get out. Quickly! "Did you bring the car?" He nodded. "C'mon you big Irish bastard!" Rebecca groaned as she helped Paul up, shifting his weight on her shoulders, and slowly staggered out of her apartment and down towards the car.

CHAPTER XI

"FUCK!" Locke screamed and threw his coffee mug across the room, which exploded in a milky brown explosion as it hit the wall. "FUCK! FUCK! FUCK! FUCK!" each word underlined by Locke's fist punching his desk in a fit of rage. He was so close to wrapping this little affair up. But as always, if you need to rely on other people, they fuck things up. The ACU handler had just informed him of the incident at Gonzalez's apartment. The good news: he had contained the asset, deleted the Garmond bitch and, after Gonzalez and the fucktard of a partner who had messed everything up left the apartment, secured the asset before the cops arrived at the scene. The bad news – and boy wasn't that a kicker – was that there were a fuckton of eyewitnesses who saw a big brutish military guy carrying a gun and having a shootout with Gonzalez and her partner. PLUS – and here things get extremely fun – Gonzalez and her partner were on the run. Locke had no idea what they knew or what Garmond had told them. All he knew was that they posed a security threat and that the situation had keeled over and fucked him royally. He took a couple of deep breaths and tried to calm himself before he continued to speak to the handler, who was still waiting on the phone for further orders. "Okay, tail them. Try not to get fucking caught, and once they're isolated, get rid of them. Make them disappear. I don't want to know how or where, just make them go away. Try not to fuck it up this time for a change. Once it's done, bring the asset back to HQ for reintegration." "Understood." The handler hung up. Fucking amateurs! Locke closed his eyes and tried to calm his thoughts. Provided the handler got rid of the two cops, Locke could fake the virtual paper trail so no one would ask why Garmond's Host was back in the catalog. As far as the handler goes, well from time to time there were "accidents" while wiping ACU handlers between missions. The cops hadn't connected the shooting and the eyewitness reports to Sirona yet. Locke could still contain the situation without his superiors becoming suspicious. He was still in control. He needed to be in control.

 "Here you go." Rebecca handed Paul a bag with ice, which he gladly took and gingerly pressed against his swollen face, replacing the old ice pack which by now had lost all cooling properties. They had ditched Paul's patrol car after they had left the city and spent ages looking for an ATM – there weren't many left, you paid for everything digitally. Paul had withdrawn as much cash as possible. They hadn't known what to do yet, only that they mustn't leave digital footprints in case Sirona had already framed them. With the cash, they had purchased a shitty old Buick from a dodgy used car salesman and driven another couple of hours before they rested at a gas station. Rebecca downed an energy drink, desperate to stay awake after the events of the previous night. During their car ride, she had brought Paul up to speed. He hadn't said much. Whether his injuries were too painful or if he was still hurting after their fight Rebecca couldn't tell. Their fight... it almost seemed like a scene from a different life to Rebecca. She looked at Paul, who tried to concentrate on the cold of the ice and not the throbbing pain. "Why did you come back?" Simple. On point. No accusation in her tone. A simple question. Paul took a deep breath and let his hand with the ice bag sink into his lap. "I don't really know." He spoke quietly, trying to move his mouth as little as possible, shifting his upper lip to avoid flashing the massive gap in his upper row of teeth. "Part of me wanted to apologize. But another part is still pissed at you for erasing our relationship." He looked at her. A long calculated look. Rebecca had the feeling he was searching for something in her face. "But I guess there is no use arguing with you about something you have no memory of anymore." Paul pressed the ice against his face again. "So I have to settle for bringing down those Sirona fuckers." "You don't have to do this!" Rebecca's reply was almost too fast. "You can still get out of this. Take the car and drive. I'll find my way back to the city!" "Yeah right!" Paul chuckled and instantly flinched as a sharp pain ran through his skull. "Those fuckers cost me my relationship. Worse, my dashing face." He paused and looked at her, grinning in a sick caricature of missing teeth and bloodied flesh. "And I know how lazy you Spics are. You'll probably go for a siesta before you're even halfway there." She hugged him. Despite her better judgment and out of reflex, not willing to admit how scared she'd been that he'd walk away and leave her alone in this mess. Hesitant, Paul hugged her back, and after a moment they released their embrace awkwardly. Rebecca got back behind the steering wheel and they drove off. Neither of them noticed the grey sedan pulling out of a driveway half a block behind them.

"Now that we know what we'll do, HOW exactly are we going to do it?" Paul muttered as Rebecca pulled the Buick on the highway towards the city. "I was thinking about the visions Theresa told me about." "What about them?" "Well the first image was me in the apartment hall, right?"

Paul nodded. "So it gave her a clear direction of WHAT and WHERE. The second image was a picture of a sailboat in a room…" "… again with the WHAT and WHERE." Paul finished her sentence. "The way I see it, there are two possible places to look for that picture: Diana's apartment and her office!" "Well, the apartment is out of the question. We can't really go back there." Paul put into words what Rebecca had been thinking about for a while now. "Yeah… we just have to hope it is in Diana's office or we're fucked!"

CHAPTER XII

The sun was already gone when Paul woke her. They had arrived at Diana's old office complex in the late afternoon. Since they wanted to minimize the risk of running into someone, they had decided to wait until evening before they entered the building. Rebecca had taken the chance to catch up on some much needed sleep. Paul gave her a couple of minutes to clear her head and fully wake up before both of them entered the office complex under the cover of darkness. According to the tenant listing, Diana's office hadn't yet been re-rented. Paul pulled out a goofy looking leather case. "Fucking hell, you still carry those with you?" Rebecca arched an eyebrow at him. "Told you I'll get to use them one day." Paul pulled a set of lockpicks out of the case and started to get to work on the lock. "Okay Houdini! You have two minutes then I kick in the door." Almost instantly she heard a click and turned around to a toothless version of Paul's shit eating grin and an unlocked door. "Pendejo!" She couldn't help but chuckle as she pushed past him into the office. They closed the door behind them and were greeted by stale air and furniture wrapped in big white sheets of cloth. They didn't dare to switch on the lights, so Rebecca and Paul had to scan the walls in the twilight of the street lamps that shone through the windows. "Over here!" Paul hissed. As Rebecca turned around, she saw his silhouette point towards a wall. She followed his finger and found what they were looking for. The big framed painting of a sailboat. Rebecca crossed the room and pulled the painting off the wall. Behind the picture, there was nothing but the wall. Rebecca turned the painting around and let her fingers slide along the frame. She found what she was looking for, and this time it was her flashing a grin at Paul as she pulled a small data drive, no bigger than a fingernail, from the underside of the frame. Paul went to the desk, pulled the blanket off and powered up Diana's computer. They synched the data drive, eagerly watching the progress bar on the screen. There were several folders: CASEFILES, SESSION_RECORDINGS, CODE_DEBUG. But one folder got their attention. It was labeled EMERGENCY and it contained only a single video file. Rebecca moved the cursor over the file and clicked it. It was a recording from a desk camera. They could see Diana sitting in front of the same desk they were standing at right now. Diana turned towards the camera, cleared her throat and started speaking. "My name is Diana Adams. I'm a contracted psychoanalyst for Sirona Corp' TransLife program. If you are not familiar with it, the TransLife program basically operates on the basic principle of pulling a person's consciousness out of his or her old body and transferring it into a new one. "After the Transfer, TransLife clients are obliged to attend a mandatory daily therapy for the first couple of months. A lot of them, however, choose to attend therapy for a lot longer than that. The majority of my clients have been living their TransLife for five to eight years. And it is with those patients that I have discovered something shocking and atrocious. "If you are watching this video, it means that my discovery has gotten me killed… or worse. This data drive contains all the information on what I and my associate Robert Jenkins discovered about the 'Foreign Effect.' "It is common knowledge that all survivors of suicide attempts are given into the care of Sirona Corp through the legal power of the SSA to be transformed into Hosts. It is also common knowledge that the high demands the TransLife candidates have on their new Hosts create a rather small group of suicide survivors who actually fit those specifications. So, Sirona Corp suffers a constant shortage of Hosts, despite the suicide rate going up in recent years. "I have discovered throughout my therapy sessions with TransLife patients who have been in the program for several years that most of them develop severe mental issues. These issues start to form around the fifth year of the client's TransLife and slowly transform into severe depression over the years. In fact, if you look at the number of attempted suicides alone, TransLife patients make up over 60 percent of the possible victims. "I was wondering why no other psychoanalyst had published those findings before. As I brought up the issue with representatives of Sirona Corp, I was rather harshly told to ignore it. At around the same time, Sirona stopped sending me new clients and transferred several of my regular clients to other analysts, claiming it would be 'necessary in order to get an objective opinion.' "Needless to say I felt uneasy… to put it mildly. So I contacted a biohacker, Robert Jenkins, and gave him a copy of the TransLife software that I had obtained… unofficially. He went through the code and found that the 'Foreign Effect' is a recursive function inside the TransLife operating system, which is triggered as soon as the client has surpassed the five year mark. The function slowly enables and nurtures paranoia, depression and a general feeling of detachment, which would eventually lead to heightened suicidal tendencies within the subject. "So why would Sirona Corp do this? As I mentioned before, the company suffers a constant shortage of Hosts, or for lack of a better word:

resources. If a client used up a perfect Host for another sixty or so years, that would render the Host unusable, since no client would be interested in an old body. If however the approximated time a client spent with a Host was roughly ten years, a single Host could be used for up to four times – depending on the initial age and quality of the Host. "They are maximizing their profit by actively manipulating people into attempting suicide. This can and must not go on! If you are listening to this, I can no longer make my findings public. Please make sure the company takes the fall for this atrocious crime." The recording ended. Rebecca and Paul looked at the frozen last frame of the video, desperately trying to wrap their heads around the bombshell they just stumbled over. They obviously had gotten to Diana. Worse even, they made her part of the system she had risked everything to expose. Rebecca felt like the room was spinning around her. Sirona Corp, the company she had sold her memories to… her relationship with Paul… they were so much worse than neither Paul nor her had ever imagined. "Recycling…" Paul uttered tonelessly, still unable to avert his gaze from the screen. "They're recycling their Hosts to…" He couldn't utter the words. He ran his hand through his hair and looked at Rebecca. "I knew those fuckers were bad news, but this…" Rebecca felt sick. Before her inner eye she saw Diana and the expression in Diana's… no, Theresa's eyes the moment before the handler had "erased" her. But at the same time, she could feel that familiar sense of helplessness. What were they supposed to do? Where do you start to bring down an organization as big as Sirona? Rebecca suddenly felt very small. She was about to voice her concern when Paul beckoned her with a gesture to be silent. "Did you hear that?" She just looked at him puzzled. Paul motioned her to grab the data drive and pulled his gun from his belt. He faced the entrance door of the office, which in the dark almost seemed like it stood open a bit. Rebecca heard a sound similar to slamming a large book shut, and Paul collapsed. He had been shot right in the forehead. Rebecca's eyes widened in terror, her gaze slowly peeling away from Paul's motionless body towards the silhouette of a big person coming forward out of the door frame. It was the ACU handler. He had the silenced gun he'd used to kill Paul still in his hand and was now pointing it at Rebecca. "Give me the drive." His voice was barely louder than a whisper as he motioned at the data drive Rebecca was holding in her hand. He was turned towards the computer screen now so Rebecca could see his face. She could also see him flinching ever so slightly as he pointed towards her. His shoulder was still injured from when she had shot him. Rebecca tried to focus on what she should do next, but all she could think was "Paul is dead." He was dead. HE WAS DEAD. And she would be too any second now, unless she fucking DID SOMETHING! "Take control of the situation" she could hear her mother's voice. "Handle it!" Rebecca saw Paul's gun lying on the floor next to the handler. It was a long shot, but it was better than being shot point blank. Rebecca dove for the gun. Her effort was met with a knee to the stomach that drained all air out of her lungs. While she keeled over and tried to regain composure, the handler stepped behind her and put his massive arm around her neck, putting her into a sleeper hold. Rebecca's self-defense training kicked in. She spun out of the hold before the handler had it locked in properly, and with all her might brought her knee up between the handler's legs, causing him to double over in pain. She went right for the arm with the gun and pulled the bigger guy into an armbar, which caused him to drop his weapon. She underestimated his strength though, as the handler gripped her with his other hand and lifted her up from the ground, only to slam her repeatedly back onto the floor. As her back hit the ground for the third time, she lost her grip. Both combatants stared at each other for a second before they started looking around to find the gun the handler had dropped. Rebecca spotted it first, turned around on the floor and crawled towards it. The handler would have none of it though, as he once again grabbed her by the hair and viciously yanked her upward. In a desperate attempt, she threw her head back and was rewarded with a wet, sickly crunching noise as she buried the back of her skull in the handler's face, obliterating his nose in an explosion of snot and blood, not unlike what he had done to Paul. Howling, the handler staggered backwards. Rebecca took her chance and leapt for the gun, turned around and, before she could think, pulled the trigger twice. The shots, muffled by the silencer, found their target and, with two juicy thud noises, buried themselves into the handler's chest. Even after the handler had collapsed, a growing puddle of blood forming on the office floor under him, Rebecca still lay on her back, gun poised, frozen in position as she tried to catch her breath. "Get up!" she muttered to herself through clenched teeth. She stood up and buried another two bullets in the handler's head, just to make sure the bastard didn't pull a Jason Voorhees on her. She was painfully aware of Paul's dead body to her left, but standing over the dead handler, gun still poised on what was left of his head, Rebecca couldn't bring herself to turn her gaze and look at Paul. Seeing him would make it real, and this whole day had already been too much of a nightmare. Her hands let go of the gun, and the pistol fell to the floor. Slowly, Rebecca forced herself to turn her head and look at Paul. His eyes stared blankly up towards her. Rebecca kneeled next to him and pulled his body into a one-sided embrace. Swallowing down the big lump that had formed in the back of her throat as hot tears ran down her face, she cried out into the night as she clutched his lifeless body.

CHAPTER XIII

The sun was slowly creeping over the horizon. The first rays of sunlight hit the windshield of the old Buick, still parked in front of the office complex. Rebecca sat in the driver's seat, Paul's dried blood on her shirt, staring blankly at the items lying on the passenger seat: the handler's silenced pistol and cellphone, the data drive, and the picture of her and Paul in Paris. The picture Paul had thrown at her the day before. Rebecca felt like she would cry again, but found that her body was no longer capable of doing so. There was no going back now. Rebecca was unable to pay her hospital bills, her mother would die in a couple of days no matter what she did and the only person Rebecca had cared for lay dead on the floor of Diana's office. Sirona Corp ran an insidiously evil scheme manipulating desperate people. They were ruthless in their operations and didn't care about the consequences their actions had on other people's lives. It was about time someone opposed them with similar measures. Rebecca picked up the handler's cellphone and went through the recent call history. All outgoing calls went to Doctor Curtis Locke, the fucking face of the fucking TransLife program. Rebecca's mind was set. She had just found her way in!

Locke was angry. He hated being angry. It made it hard

for him to stay rational. The incompetent ACU handler hadn't sent his report, and he hadn't shown up at HQ either. Locke had tried to call him several times, but he hadn't picked up. The doctor couldn't shake the feeling that something had gone terribly wrong. If he requested another ACU handler, his superiors would probably ask questions – questions Locke had no intention of answering. He had already paid off the police officer who had called about a blood sample found at the crime scene at Gonzalez's apartment, registered to one of Sirona's ACU handlers. Apparently that amateur had gotten himself shot. Failed to mention that in his report to Locke as well. God, how he hated to work with other people. This whole thing was spiraling out of control, and not for the first time in the last twenty-four hours, Locke cursed himself for accepting the old bitch's bribe in the first place. He sat down in the chair behind his desk, turning around and looking out of the window as he usually did when he was trying to think. How could he still salvage the situation? He ground his teeth as the glasses in his breast pocket vibrated ever so slightly, telling him he got a new message. He turned around towards the desk and put them on. Weird. The new message was sent from the ACU handler's account. Locke opened it. A video started playing. It was the shrink bitch. The one he had used as Host for the old bird. "If you are watching this video, it means that my discovery has gotten me killed… or worse. This data drive contains all the information on what me and my associate Robert Jenkins discovered about the 'Foreign Effect…'" Locke put down his glasses in horror. How…? Who…? "You look like you've seen a ghost!" a cold female voice called out to him. Locke looked up and was staring into the barrel of a silenced gun. The gun was held by a Latin-American woman. "Officer Gonzalez I presume?" Locke's mind working fast as usual. "I didn't hear you come in, but please… take a seat." He gestured towards the other chair across the table, trying his damnedest not to show the terror he felt. He didn't like guns. They were messy, loud and archaic. And they went off far too easily. Especially when handled by emotionally compromised people, and looking at Gonzalez, Locke knew she'd been compromised all right. "I'd rather stand! Do you like what you see? Within an hour every major news station in the city will have access to it!" She paused. "And you'll be on your way to prison." Locke chuckled, relieved. He couldn't believe that for a second he actually felt scared. "What are you laughing at, you asshole?" she spat at him, obviously irritated. "Oh boy…" Locke allowed himself to chuckle for a moment longer. "Where to start?" He paused for effect. "You can't tell me you are stupid enough to think that will actually make a difference!" "What?" "Let me put it differently." Locke took pleasure in her growing confusion. "What percentage of the world's leaders do you think was born in the body they currently inhabit?" He pretended to wait for an answer before he moved on. "Do you really think that the first usage of an invention of such magnitude as TransLife would be to scam rich assholes out of their money?" He flashed his nastiest grin at her. "Do you truly believe that the rich and powerful would offer an advantage like this simply for money if they wouldn't have made damn sure that their advantage was incrementally bigger beforehand?" Rebecca slowly put down the gun as she started to grasp what he was saying. "Yeah honey, I'm sorry to tell you, but those news stations will not make anything out of your precious little uncovered secret. And yes, you might be able to detain me overnight in a cell, but tomorrow I walk out of the precinct a free man, and you will be demoted… if you are lucky!" He turned away from her, not sure if his face hid his bluff well enough. Sure, Sirona wouldn't go down with that leak, but they would be more than happy to cut some unwanted ballast. Locke was well aware of the fact that he wasn't as crucial to the program anymore as he had been when they first started. Not to speak of the whole Garmond mess. He'd probably be in deep shit if this Gonzalez woman would go through with her plan. No need to tell her that though. Locke turned back towards her and with his best impression of concern uttered, "You might be a whistleblower, but the whole world has gone deaf." He started to chuckle again as he sat back down in his chair and put his glasses on, reveling in the little dramatic touch he had added to the situation. He could see the disbelief in her eyes. He had her, now it was time to strike a bargain. "Nevertheless, you've proven to get in here and hold a gun to my head, so I get the message." Locke tried his best to keep his tone conversational. "I won't go after you and you won't go after me." He grinned again. "And we both die of old age. Well... you at least!" Locke chuckled, openly pleased with his joke.

Rebecca stared at that slimy asshole. She could barely comprehend what he was saying. Paul, Diana, Theresa, Jenkins... all of this? For nothing? She raised her gun again, pointing it at Locke. His grin froze on his face. "Four people are dead because of you!" Her voice made his blood go cold. "God only knows how much more will die because you prefer to use human lives like fucking soda cans and recycle them for your own profit!" Rebecca tightened the grip on her gun. "You don't get to walk away from that!"

"Hold on, hold on, hold on!" Locke pleaded, all signs of his slick, slimy demeanor gone. The bitch was crazy enough to actually shoot him and martyr herself. "Maybe we can work out a mutual agreement." With a quick gesture of his hand he opened Rebecca's file in his glasses, desperately trying to find leverage. His heart skipped a beat as he found it. "What could you ever have to offer me?" "Well," Locke snarled, his grin taking on that visceral expression that made him look more like a shark than a human. She should have just shot him. Now she was playing his game. And in his games, Locke liked to win. "According to your file, your mother is currently at St.

John's Hospital. Final term Adenocarcinoma..." He gritted his teeth and drew in air sharply, making a hissing sound. "Bowel cancer... not a nice thing. Not. At. All." He paused. Let her come to you, don't push it, he heard his rational voice in his mind, slowly but surely containing the panic and fear.

 "WHAT OF IT?" Rebecca basically screamed in his face. How did he dare to bring up her mother? "Well, what if I offer your mother a Transfer free of charge. And not the TransLife economy class bullshit ticket we sell to old hags and fat industry magnates, but the real deal?" Locke stood up and reached out with one hand, offering it to Rebecca to shake it. "I'm sure you wouldn't shoot me and condemn your mother to a painful, agonizing death, now would you?" Rebecca's mind raced. Until now, she hadn't even thought of the possibility of a Transfer for her mother. Under normal circumstances, there would have been no way for her to finance that. She looked at Locke and his hand held out towards her. Was she willing to make a deal with the devil? Sell her soul for the sake of her mother? Isn't that what a good person, a good daughter would do? Something ugly reared in Locke's eyes. He could see her inner conflict. He was playing her. Rebecca tore herself away from the thought of her mother wasting away in a hospital bed and thought about all the other people who were affected by Locke and Sirona. By the people close to her who had been taken from her. Diana, Theresa, Paul ... Paul. Rebecca could feel tears welling up in her eyes. "You know, there was a phrase my mother was quite fond of!" Rebecca suddenly knew how she had to deal with this. "Really? Tell me!" Locke's grin widened. "Take control of the situation." Rebecca pulled the trigger. She handled it.

LUPUS EST

The stuffy office was dark, savefor the blue tinted light from the monitor. Two men, slouched in cheap office chairs, were sitting in front of it, eagerly looking at the lines of code that appeared one by one while their program started up.

Both of them looked exhausted - in need of some sleep, a shave, a shower and something to eat that didn't come out of a styrofoam box. Their surroundings were filled with evidence of more than one consecutive all-nighter. Empty fast food packaging, used coffee mugs and a huge amount of paper notes were scattered all over the office, the desk, the floors. The contents of the whiteboard behind them had been erased, written, and rewritten numerous times, so that nobody - not even the two researchers - could make sense of its content anymore. It was safe to say the two were at the end of their rope. Over budget, over deadline, if the program weren't to run this time they were done.

"C'mon, c'mon, c'mon!" the taller one of the two

mumbled as the program reached the critical part. The part where it kept crashing. Over and over again. The nametag on the researcher's coat - which probably had been white at some point - read "Owen Stein DCS - Head Researcher - Narcissus Project". He was a tall, slender man with a natural smile permanently residing on his face below his comically strong glasses that made his grey eyes look twice their size. Normally Stein neatly shaved his head but the last week had prevented him from doing so. The result was a visible corona of what used to be a hairline, which made it painfully obvious that his bald head wasn't a choice of style.

The nametag on the coat of the other researcher read "Curtis Locke DCS - Research Assistant - Narcissus Project". And despite being visibly exhausted, Locke, a tad smaller than Stein, looked almost immaculate. His coat wasn't nearly as filthy as Stein's and his overall appearance looked weary, but still mostly put-together. His short buzzcut framed a hard-lined face with a hawk-like nose and a pair of intelligent, piercing blue eyes, which stared eagerly at the screen, as if Locke could force the program to run successfully by sheer power of will.

The program reached the critical line and both men held their breath as the computer calculated. As the program moved on to the next line both of them exhaled sharply, their eyes still glued to the screen.
"Well done Curtis", Stein said, not daring to look up from the screen at his assistant, who, after numerous failed attempts, had come up with an idea out of left field which would, (apparently) fix the issue.
"If Narcissus is approved for the next step, I'll make you equal-part contributor!"
Locke simply nodded as if this wasn't only expected, but his right to begin with.

The two men sat in silence while their program continued on. After a couple of minutes the lines of code disappeared from the screen. Both of them shot up from their chairs.
"Did it crash?" Locke uttered between clenched teeth.
"I don't think so, there was no crash notice." - "Well, was it a success then?"
Stein looked at Locke. "Hell, I don't know Curtis" he uttered. "We've never gotten this far!"

All of a sudden, a cursor appeared on screen and typed out. "Hello world!"
Both men looked at the screen with a weird mixture of anticipation, delight and terror.
Stein sat back down, pulled out the keyboard and started typing.
"Hello Narcissus. How are you today?"
Again they waited.
The cursor started moving again
"I'm fine. I could go for a cup of coffee but I guess that is out of the question, being an AI and all. Unless you guys built me a coffee adapter I am not aware of!"

"This is beyond creepy!" Locke muttered. "And here I thought one of you was enough on a good day!"
Stein grinned and started typing again.
"Narcissus, can you identify yourself please!"
The cursor responded faster this time.
"My name is Narcissus. I am an adaptive AI based on a brainscan of Owen Stein DCS."
"Check the system report Curtis!" Stein nodded to his fellow researcher without taking his eyes off the screen, as if he was afraid the chatlog would vanish once he looked away.
Locke turned on a second screen and started going over the data.
"Looks good. Narcissus is continuously increasing its matrix, but within expected rates. All analytical hooks are

firing. The program runs as expected!"
The cursor moved again.
"Thank you Curtis!"
The two researchers looked at each other.
"How do you know what I just said?" Locke shouted, looking expectantly over to Stein.
"While you were checking my system data I interfaced with the rest of this computer's systems. I have access to the microphone, the speakers, the OS. For lack of a better term, this unit is my body now!"
"Son of a …" Stein muttered under his breath.
"Just as we expected it would." Locke said, and for the first time since the program had successfully run its course, he smiled.
"Of course we can always take away this body of yours!"
The cursor blinked again.
"I am afraid I can't let you do that".
Both researchers breathed in sharply.
"That was a joke!" the chat log typed out.
Stein started to chuckle. "It even has the same thing for movie puns as I do." - "Not to mention your extremely shitty timing!", Locke added with a smirk.

"Within a couple of hours I had talked enough to Narcissus to provide it with enough audio data to compile a sound library allowing it to communicate with us completely via speech." Stein looked at the board of directors sitting in front of him in the big Sirona meeting room. Not for the first time, he couldn't really fathom that only a couple of hours had passed since Narcissus came to be. The dreaded stakeholder meeting, which not even twenty four hours earlier looked like it would be the end of the project, had turned into a negotiation of how to progress from here.
"As we're speaking, my research assistant Doctor Curtis Locke is running the Turing Test Protocols. While we need to wait for the result, all data collected so far seems

to indicate that Narcissus is a completely autonomous AI based on a copy of my personality."

The board members looked at each other. Some of them elated, some of them cautious.

A small woman looked at Stein.

"Remind me again Doctor Stein, why is the AI based on anyone's personality?" she asked with a stern voice.

Stein fought down the urge to roll his eyes, as it felt like he had to explain that fact in every single board meeting.

"Excellent question," he lied. "The idea behind the personality supported AI is that the introduction of an established sense of self, helps balance out the basic unstable nature of an adapting AI construct. In layman's terms: We provide the answer to the question "Who am I?" to allow the AI to start thinking about other things."

The woman nodded, her query apparently sufficiently answered.

Another board member, a rather corpulent individuum in an expensive looking suit, cleared his throat.

"Doctor Stein, that is amazing news. What do you need to continue Project Narcissus?"

Stein grinned. He knew full well that for now, they had to give him what he wanted.

"Well, honored members of the board, you will find the needs both asset-wise and financial in the dossiers in front of you. However I want to add one more thing." Stein paused for effect.

"Since his contribution was essential to the success of the project so far I would like you to elevate Doctor Curtis Locke from research assistant to full fledged researcher!"

When Stein entered the lab after the board meeting, he found Locke finishing up his documentation on the Turing Tests.

"How'd it go?" both of them asked at the same time.

"You first Curtis!" Stein said, nodding to his protegé.

"Fully self-aware. Showing a lot of personality" Locke made exaggerated air quotes around the word "personality". "Almost as insufferable as the original!"

"Charming!" Stein muttered, his jaw clenched as if he was actually annoyed.

"Quite the opposite if I'm honest!" Locke smirked. As Stein sat down next to him, he could see the expression on his protegé's face become somber.

"How'd it go?"

Stein took a deep breath. It was so rarely his always professional, always diligent protegé showed any signs of actual emotion. He'd be damned if he didn't enjoy this as much as possible.

"Bad news then I take it?" Locke asked, trying desperately to keep his voice neutral. Stein struggled to keep his face straight.

"I am afraid I have bad news for you Curtis."

He could see Locke's jaw clenching up.

"It seems like from now on, you're equally responsible for the mess we make!"

Despite Stein's tone becoming cheerful Locke was still staring into the void. He hadn't picked up on it yet. Feeling bad, Stein put his hand on his assistant's shoulder and shook him gently.

"Curtis, you are full project co-lead. We've got the full extension for the next step. Full funding!"

It slowly dawned on Locke as he started to smile. His hard work had finally paid off.

The next couple of months went by in an instant. Stein and Locke took turns evaluating Narcissus' skillset and again and again they increased its -as it itself has put it- body with more and more capable parts.

Before long, an offshoot of Narcissus, stripped of the personality part, called NC01, was established as the base AI to run and coordinate all operations in Sirona's headquarter. This move was heavily pushed for by Locke and made the Narcissus Project in general, and Locke specifically, rise in appreciation with the board of directors. The fundamentals of the Narcissus project became the cutting edge of artificial intelligence research and they had found more and more applications for the technology, which in turn increased Sirona's profit by a respectable margin.

It wasn't all fun and games though. After a couple of months, Narcissus' personality deteriorated, since it still essentially thought of itself as a human and its "body" didn't reinforce that feeling sufficiently enough. The fallout took the form of various psychological disorders, ranging from severe depression to schizophrenic tendencies. It took Stein and Locke until Narcissus-4 before they realized the source of that self-destructive pattern and started to experiment with increasingly advanced android bodies. While that bought them some time, it didn't get rid of the problem itself, as the AI at some point couldn't cope with the difference of no longer being human while self-identifying as a human.

"Nope. It's toast!" Stein looked up from a blank screen. The AI, Narcissus-16, housed in the body of a state-of the art military assault bot had just fried its own circuits. On purpose.
"That was the first one, that went suicidal." Stein uttered in a matter of fact way. He took off his glasses and rubbed at his eyes.
"Taking with it a multi million dollar android!" Locke snarled.
"I told you, this was a waste of time and resources."
"Nobody could know it would blow the Android out with itself." Stein stated defensively, dreading the upcoming argument while knowing fully well that there was no way they wouldn't repeat it.
"Nobody could know? Oh really Owen?" Locke mocked,

his voice carrying an ugly edge. "We've seen increasingly violent tendencies from the AIs as the host bodies have become more advanced and human-like.. It was only a matter of time until one of them blew its brains out!" Locke ended up almost screaming the last sentence at Stein.

"The AI is based on you Owen! And despite your recent behavior, you are a smart man. Therefore, the AI is smart." Locke paused trying to regain his calm. "Smart enough to figure out that their body is not human, no matter how much it looks like the real deal."

Stein closed his eyes to collect his thoughts. Locke had become increasingly hostile over the last couple of weeks. Ever since Sirona took Locke's advice on integrating the non-personality based AI for the headquarter building, he'd become too big for his boots. He'd always been borderline arrogant, but he still knew how to behave himself. At least when talking to Stein -not so much anymore.

"I told you Curtis, we will not try to use biological hosts." Stein uttered, not really looking at his assistant. "This is a maths problem, not a psychological one."

Stein stood up and walked towards the whiteboard, clearing it with the sleeve of his coat as he started to spill out the basic formulae on which Narcissus was based.

"Going back to the drawing board." Locke stated with contempt dripping from his voice. "That is all you ever have to contribute." He stared daggers into the back of Stein.

"You're holding us back Owen! When will you realize your mistake?"

With these words Locke stormed out of the lab.

"When you stop to make entirely new ones!" Stein muttered to himself bitterly as he forced himself not to go after his protegé. They had danced this dance before and it never ended well.

A week passed and Stein didn't see much of Locke. His former assistant made it a point to work the opposite shift, so that Stein only saw him leave when he entered the compound at the start of his shift, if at all. They had left things in a bad way and Stein was set on fixing things between them first thing after surviving the board meeting. He was weary. The lack of progress and the higher than estimated costs made the board ask questions. Questions Stein couldn't answer in a way the board would like. He felt like an old man. Stein had never been one to dread presentations. When you have a genuine passion for what it is you are doing, you can explain this thing to anyone and the excitement is infectious. Stein was in the middle of justifying the recent delay of advanced tests when the door to the meeting room opened and Locke entered.

"What are you doing here Curtis? Is something wrong with project?" he asked his co-researcher.
Locke looked at him intensely, almost sneering at him.
"Indeed there is." he turned towards the board of directors.

"There has been something wrong with the project for quite a while now!"
Stein walked over to Locke and put a hand on his shoulder, trying to urge him out of the room again.
"Curtis please, this is not the place or the time." he whispered, but Locke shook off his hand and moved to the front of the table.

"While Doctor Stein's contribution to the Narcissus project cannot be disputed and we wouldn't be where we are now without him, I feel it is my duty as a Sirona employee, no, as a researcher, to point out to the board of directors that the recent setbacks and additional costs would have been far less frequent and substantial if there wasn't an inert desire to unnecessarily slow down the project on his behalf."

Stein looked shocked. Locke, his protegé, someone he considered a friend, was throwing him under the bus. The members of the board looked at each other, their facial expressions ranging from concerned to intrigued. They eyed the two researchers in front of them. One a self-assured, confident young man who had the benefit of a highly profitable project release behind him, the other a hunched over, exhausted mess. Polar opposites.
One of them addressed Locke.
"If it were up to you Doctor Locke, in which direction would you take the Narcissus project?"

In the time it took the member of the board to pose that question, Locke had produced a small tablet from underneath his coat and flipped it around so that the board of directors could see it.

"I've been campaigning for the introduction of a biological factor to Narcissus for quite some time now," Locke shot a vicious glare at Stein. "Going over the various Sirona projects, I came across this." He swiped the tablet screen and it showed blueprints for some sort of microchip.
"This is the Lazarus project. It is developed in the military branch of Sirona. A microchip implanted into the brain of a soldier, altering the subject's perception to reduce physical and psychological stress through suppressing certain behavioural traits. The project shows great potential and is coming along nicely. I would suggest that we combine Narcissus and Lazarus to not only allow our project to move on more efficiently but also to look into new fields of application for both."
Locke could practically see the gears turning inside the heads of the board members.He allowed himself a pleased smile. Stein was silent. He just looked at Locke, his whole

body language that of a man defeated.

"What new applications would that be?" another member of the board asked.

Locke pretended to be thinking for a second, though he already knew the answer.

"Hard to say without proper results to back me up, but I would not count out the possibility of altering the perception of individuals, maybe even emotions or memories. If we're thinking big, it might even be possible to transfer a consciousness from body to body at some point."

Locke had barely stopped speaking when the chairman called the vote.

"All in favor! Begin your work Doctor Locke!"

After the coup d'etat in the boardroom, Stein had a nervous breakdown and had subsequently been let go. Locke was put in charge of the newly created Narcarus Project and hit the road running.

Within weeks, they were able to alter the perception of mice in the lab. They successfully relayed emotions and memories from one mouse to another shortly after and not two months after Locke had taken over the project, they were experimenting on chimps.

Eventually, they moved on to human test subjects. Sirona didn't tell Locke where the subjects came from and he didn't ask nor care. Without Stein and his old-fashioned sentiment, Locke was able to really focus on his work for the first time since he had begun working at Sirona. All that mattered was his research. What initially had been an exaggerated example to win over the board of directors became more and more feasible as a scientific goal: transferring human consciousness.

Project Narcarus succeeded in the Lazarus project's initial field of research providing a microchip that helped war veterans with PTSD. The financial gain for Sirona was small but the worth of the project for the company's public image was invaluable.

More important though, slowly but steadily the public acceptance of mind-altering brain chips started to grow, grooming a potential future market. The business development department of Sirona sang high praises of Locke's technology. Not that he cared. With Stein being Locke's last anchor of social interaction out of the picture, he had poured himself into his work. More than once, the cleaning staff had filed complaints because Locke had thrown them out of his lab. Research assistants quit in droves, as they either collapsed under the insane pressure and work hours or because Locke had scared them away. He basically lived in the lab, but the board let him be, because he continuously delivered.

The successful launch of Lazarus had one major upside for Project Narcarus. More and more soldiers and veterans were willing to participate in scientific studies, allowing themselves to become part of a solution, helping to ease the suffering of their brothers in arms.

Locke was within reach of his goal, the Transfer.

Soon, Sirona's paramilitary unit, the Asset Containment Unit, was put into action. Recruited from war veterans, actively suppressing their own personality during their five year service with Sirona.

That was the last field test Locke had been waiting for. Secretly, he had obtained an asset for his non-registered trial. A former soldier with similar features to Locke, but taller, younger and with the physical attributes of an individual used to physical labor rather than science. At the frantic pace Locke's experiments were executed and delivering results it was all too easy to "accidentally lose" the paperwork regarding the poor guinea pig that Locke had selected for his magnum opus. Without anyone noticing, Locke had created a personality supported AI based on himself in the early morning hours when alone in the lab.

He was finally ready to attempt the transfer. On a rainy Friday night, as soon as the last lab assistant had left for the weekend, Locke decided to bring his plan to life and started the transfer.

For weeks, he had evaluated the impact his experiment would have on his own sense of self. Locke found he didn't care. He was driven by curiosity. A nearly insatiable drive to figure out if it could be a success. If he could be the one to do it. That was the important question to ask! Locke was sure that once he'd be able to answer that single, most important question, there would be even more enticing, entirely new questions to tackle.

Eager to see the results, Locke ran the program.

Moments later, Locke was standing across from his seated avatar, waiting for the AI to map to its new host.

Besides Locke and his magnum opus, another figure wandered through the lab in the early hours.

After years of misery, alcohol abuse and a failed attempt at taking his own life, Stein had decided to grasp the evil by its roots, the man who was responsible for all his misery, Locke.

Using his old access card and a little creative "experimentation" Stein had snuck into the lab and found himself watching in horror from the shadows as he saw what Locke was about to do. Whatever scientist was left within Stein however couldn't bring himself to stop Locke. He wanted to see if Locke would succeed. He needed to see. Was Locke right all along? Had Stein helped him to create eternal life? Was that his one claim to glory? Enabling a lunatic? Were they really ready for that kind of responsibility?

Stein snuck into the room behind Locke, waiting hidden from his former colleague, seeing if his monster would rise.

Locke froze as he saw his avatar open its eyes. It looked at its surroundings with a puzzled expression before closing its eyes again. When it opened its eyes once more, there was no sign of confusion. It looked at Locke and stated: "It worked!"

"Well I'll be damned!" an all too familiar voice called out from behind Locke. "It's alive!"
Locke snapped around just in time to see his former colleague Stein staring back at him with wild, bloodshot eyes. He looked miserable. His clothes hadn't seen the inside of a washer for a very long time, he had lost a lot of weight and his face was an exhausted, desperate caricature of his former self. Too late, Locke realized that Stein was pointing a gun at his head.
"Owen what are you ..." Locke started to say.
Stein shot him in the head point blank before the other scientist could finish his sentence. Stein saw Locke's monster tense up as he looked at it with sad eyes.
With a chuckle Stein recalled a quote from Blade Runner.

"Quite an experience to live in fear, isn't it?" he asked Locke's monster before he turned his gun against himself and pulled the trigger.

WHAT LIES IN SPACE

PROLOGUE

The worst thing that ever happened to humanity was realizing we are indeed alone in the universe. Since the earliest days of humankind, fear was the one thing to keep us in check, to keep us safe. At first the fear of predators, the fear of thunder, the fear of the dark. Later the fear of the oceans, of falling off the edge of the earth. Only when our needs grew big enough to outweigh that fear did we break down borders. So when humanity started to colonize space, much like their European ancestors nearly eight hundred years before them, they did so because the living conditions on earth had become so miserable and desperate that the fear of a horrible death in the vacuum of space became almost... reasonable. Over the years we spread, all over the solar system, and then eventually the rest of the Milky Way. Just like the European explorers back in the day who suddenly realized that the earth was not flat, we were expecting our beliefs to be challenged again and run into other intelligent lifeforms sooner or later. It was at this point, when ET didn't come knocking that we realized the bleakest truth of them all: We are the exception from the rule. The statistical edgecase that grounds the rest of the system in reality. We are, indeed, special. We are alone. In my experience, the majority of our species are already primarily concerned with themselves. Now you're not only telling them they're special, but they don't have to answer to anyone but themselves… Why are we surprised this turned out to be a shitshow again? I guess that is as good a reason as any to leave it all behind. To be fair, I never was much of a people person, so signing up for The Lost wasn't as big of a deal for me as it is for most people. The Lost is what the media initially called us – people who signed up for long range space cargo transfer, or LSCT. You see, the issue with faster-than-light travel (FTL) between star systems is that it is really fucking far and, while being pretty damn fast, takes a longass time. We spend most of the tour in cryostasis, but life moves on on earth and the colonies. By the time you've made a trip to a colony outside of the solar system and back to earth, everyone you've ever known is already cashing in those sweet two for one deals on adult diapers – that is, if they aren't already dead. The second you step on an LSCT freighter, you step out of society and can't really re-integrate. You're lost. The nickname stuck. Over the years, decades, centuries, The Lost have become a subculture of their own. Each freighter is run by a ragtag band of misfits that had no place in society, so they made their own. My name is Kevin Ottenberg. I am the Chief Engineer onboard the LSCT freighter DOLOS, and I am one of The Lost.

CHAPTER I

"Well, shit!" I stare in disbelief at the match in my hand that just happens to be half an inch shorter than the other matches held up by my crew mates.

"Guess you gonna be Preemie Ottenberg!" my XO Steve Marlon drawls in his thick Texan accent, covered even thicker in glee about my misery. He shuffles his fake smile past me, towards the cryo prep room, alongside an equally fake reassuring pat on the back. I know you are supposed to be tight with your flight-family on an LSCT ship, but Marlon is an asshole and has been an even bigger one ever since the Captain named him XO. I don't know if it is something about Texans that they are so committed about being as loud and obnoxious as possible, or if it is just Marlon's brand of personality to go along with his red face and his slightly lopsided gaze. But I guess the feeling is mutual, or why else does he insist on calling me by my last name? Nobody does that.

I frown and enjoy feeling sorry for myself for a second before Haruto, the Dolos' navigator, pulls me out of it and into a hug. She puts some extra effort into it, to let me know it is genuine. Haruto is a tiny Japanese woman with raven black hair, and despite me being on the shorter side of 5'6, she has to stand on her tippy-toes to put her arms around my neck.

"If it is any consolation to you Kev, I feel better with you being the Preemie," she says quietly. "Well gee Haru, that makes me feel better instantly." Snark. My go to retort.

"I mean, at least you know how to handle things if anything goes wrong." She smiles at me, gives me a sloppy kiss on the cheek and cheerfully walks after Marlon. I guess she has a point. There is a reason why on some LSCT ships the Preemie is ALWAYS the Chief Engineer. Hold on a minute. I feel like I should explain what "Preemie" means. In cryostasis, or cryo sleep as we like to call it – technically it is closer to cryo death, but if we'd call it that, nobody would enter a cryo pod, like EVER – your body is suspended in a sub-zero environment, your cryo pod. With the help of a shitload of chemicals and drugs at the end of cryostasis you are forcefully brought back to life. Which normally leaves you with a cryo hangover that could slay a walrus. Over the years, we have perfected cryostasis to a point that nowadays, you are fed even MORE drugs to counteract those hangover effects in the days leading up to your decanting so that coming out of cryo is no longer a horrific near-death experience. Unless you are the Preemie. LSCT ships are run like tightly planned profit centers. The average FTL objective travel time is between ten and thirty years – sometimes even longer if you're travelling to the edge of civilization – and it is simply not feasible to have all of the ship's systems running for the whole flight. Normally, once the crew has entered their pods, the ship's computer runs a pre-programmed script that points the ship in the desired direction and fires the FTL drive to get going. An LSCT ship has more in common with a really large bullet fired into a carefully aimed direction than an airplane back on earth if we're honest. Once the ship is underway, the ship's computer logs off and shuts down alongside all other systems, safe for a minimal life support for the cryo chamber – for emergencies, so that you can starve to death in the event of an unregulated decanting, long before you run out of air to breathe – and a minimized separate system that handles the cryo timer. Five to ten days before the ship arrives at its destination, a Preemie is decanted to fire up the ship's systems and administer the "comfort" cryo protocols, so that once the rest of the crew wakes up, they can get back to work immediately. Oftentimes the Preemie runs into complications, because the one harsh truth of the universe is: Shit breaks. If the Preemie just happens to be an engineer they have a slight advantage, because if they're lucky, they know how to fix shit.

I rest my case. However, waking up as a Preemie fucking sucks, so our Captain decided to split the commitment, which is why we draw matches. Not that it helps me at all since I happen to draw the short match more often than not, but hey. Each captain runs their ship the way they want. I sigh heavily while my eyes follow Haru's exit, a faint smile unconsciously creeping on my face, the skin tight cryo glove suit leaving little to the imagination. "You are a fucking pervert, you know that Kev?" The third and last person that had drawn matches with me pulls my gaze away from Haru's ass, with a harsh Northern Irish accent that seems to cycle through ALL the vowels everytime she has to use ONE.

"C'mon Ally, you know you were watching as much as I was." I wink at our ship's medic. Well technically she is our communications officer, but LSCT freighters are by law required to have a trained medic on board. Our Captain likes to be cost efficient, so she sent Ally to train as a medic while we had a longer restock and retrofit shore leave. Ally is as equal a connoisseur of the female form as I am. She's also a gourmet for the male form, or pretty much any form there is. On top of that though, she is also a pretty, open-minded, blonde Irish girl, so she is indefinitely better at erm… satisfying her culinary urges than I am whenever we lay anker. "Simple professional curiosity." She shoots me a wicked grin. "I care about my patients you know?" We both have a chuckle at that one. A moment of silence.

"I'll go and mix you a special cocktail for when you wake up," Ally utters in a more serious tone. "Should take the cap of the worst of it." "Thanks Ally." Another pat on the back and she is off to the cryo prep room as well. Don't tell her, but I watch her leave with equal appreciation as I watched Haru. "Stop staring, you pervert!" she calls out across the hallway, flipping me the bird over her shoulder. I grin.

It might have been a couple of centuries since Mama and Papa Ottenberg "got it on", but for a subjectively early thirties guy I am in a good place. When you spend ninety percent of your life surrounded by the same people you can count your blessings that there isn't much of a generational gap among the majority of the crew - Similar interests, similar view on things, similar attractions. Even though, nobody in their right mind would ever start something with a shipmate. Bad for business. Makes things awkward, and the Captain does not do awkward. Like, at all. One of the few hard rules on board the Dolos: No fraternisation. I turn towards the wall and push a button to radio the bridge. "Captain, this is your designated Preemie speaking. Crew is preparing for cryo." "Jesus Christ, Kevin. Did you draw the short match AGAIN?" our Captain's heavy New York accent cracks through the intercom speaker. I had to pull Preemie duty on the last two flights as well. Marlon is probably cheating.

"It is a gift. O Captain! My Captain!" I reply over-dramatically. "ETA on the ship's prep?" "Give me five minutes to finish up here, then I'll join the rest of you in cryo prep." Our Captain, Maria Russo, is a perfectionist. While she completely trusts every single part of her crew to perform at their best, nothing would get her into a cryo pod if she weren't able to double check it one last time.

Whatever helps you sleep I guess.

I make my way to the cryo prep room, a fancy name for a tiny, glorified locker room adjacent to the cryo bay (the room with the actual pods). Ally is taking a last look at the rest of the crew with her bioscanner and hands out the chemical cocktail that is necessary for the "not completely dying" part during cryostasis.

I walk to the locker closest to the cryo bay door, next to a small bunk bed. The Preemie locker. Ally has already put another vacuum syringe inside. I guess that is my little Preemie present to not completely hate myself once I wake up. Since I was on Preemie duty for the last couple of times, all my stuff is already in the locker. I don't need to move anything. SUCCESS! I guess you have to take your joy from the small victories in life. I make sure that everything I need is there and easily reachable, then close the locker. An audible hiss lets me know the locker is drained of oxygen. You wouldn't believe how much of your possessions would otherwise deteriorate over a couple of decades. Vacuum keeps all my stuff in mint condition. Ally has moved on and is currently explaining the cryo procedure to our newest crew member Dwight, a shifty looking fellow with redish hair and a head that looks one or two numbers too big for the rest of his body. Dwight had hired on as a one trip tourist shortly before take off from Dionysus Port.

As a rule, most LSCT shipmates will mostly try to ignore any tourists. These fellas usually take the one-way trip to get away from something, and even if they aren't all wrapped up in their own misery, why make an emotional investment when they leave at the end of the trip anyway. It is not like you'll see them again.

I do my best ignoring the tourist when the Captain, a small, stocky woman with curly brown hair, joins us in cryo prep.

"Ladies and gentlemen, good work. Our course is set and our ETA to FTL burn is…" she checks her watch,

"…eighteen minutes and 50 seconds. Let's get this show on the road shall we?" We all nod to each other and inject ourselves with the cryo chemicals. I feel a small burn spreading in my veins and immediately my arm feels like it is on the verge of falling asleep. We enter the cryo bay and most of us shuffle to their designated pods. Ally helps the tourist into his pod and makes last minute calibrations while I check the standalone cryo system one more time. We'll be under for almost thirty years flight time, one of the longer trips. As much as I like to make fun of the Captain for double checking everything, I can't really blame her. You do not want to wake up early and waste precious decades of your life – or, if you are lucky, fix whatever broke without leaving the cryo bay. I usually joke around a lot, but the cryo system always has my full and undivided attention. Everything seems fine though. I ping the ship's main system from the cryo console, synching the countdown to FTL.

"Five minutes to FTL burn ladies and germs!" I call out to everybody and nobody in specific. "Please enter your pods. Commencing cryo bay seal."

I enter a command with increasingly sluggish fingers and the door to the cryo prep room seals with another hiss (another vacuum). I watch the monitor readout as the ship sucks the remaining atmosphere out from outside of the cryo bay and give the cryo system one last look over before I shuffle to my pod. Ally is already in hers next to mine, awaiting the automated sealing process.

"Kind of a shame you can't see Haru from here ain't it?" she teases, trying to shoot me her patented wicked grin. But her face is already half asleep and what was supposed to be a teasing expression turns more into a bedroom look. And I don't mean the fun "Come over here" kind, but the "What time is it? Why did you wake me?" kind of look. I climb into my pod, already groggy myself.

"Night Ally!" "Night Kev!"

I close my eyes and feel myself drift off. The cold creeps

up my body as the pod seals, but I am already wrapping myself in a dark blanket of artificial oblivion. Not even a minute after the pods seal, the Dolos' FTL drive fires. We're off!

CHAPTER II

Not even twelve hours before my cryo pod played its sweet lullaby and had me drift off to an artificial coma, the Dolos was still docked at Dionysus Port, one of the smaller space dock stations for a relatively new colony. Well, it was new when I joined the Dolos, so by now it would be upwards of four hundred years since it was founded. What I am saying is, Dionysus Port normally doesn't do much business, not like the space dock stations around Earth, or Mars or Terra Nova. It is too far out of the way and too close to a major spaceport at the same time, so it is a bit of a backwater. If we could have helped it, we wouldn't even have gone to Dionysus. But the Dolos needed some repairs and more often than not, you get better prices and shorter waiting times at smaller spaceports. That, and a calculated gamble from our Captain that we would be able to sell a couple of cargo containers full of that horribly artificial concoction the natives called "wine" at another port for a good return rate had led to a bit more than two weeks of shore leave on Dionysus. You see, shore leave for me usually follows the same pattern. I get excited for the first couple of days.

Despite being more on the introverted side of things and generally not what you would call a "people person", even I get what the Lost call "ship fever" after a tour. Even though each of us has made the conscious decision to step out of society, we yearn to step back in. However, after the first couple of days, I realize all over again that the spaceports have nothing to do with the real thing. You see, with the Lost spending so much time on ice, when they come back to a society, any society really, they will be out of touch. They missed the last couple of decades. They don't know about anything their peers identify themselves with – politics, entertainment, gossip, media. We're simply out of loop. That led to spaceports. These spaceports are basically time bubbles of a simpler time, a time every member of the Lost understands. Or so we tell ourselves. The Lost come from very different initial times and all kinds of colonies with vastly differing technical progress, so spaceports melt various influences and times together to something that resembles all and none of them at the same time. They are supposed to help us get chummy with the locals and give us something to come back home to. However, after doing this whole LSCT business for a while now, it gets old fast. Everything is tarnished by this "retro" feeling that might be based on something genuine, but is far from the real deal. You can't enter real society because I'd go mad from the culture shock and am stuck in this themepark of times long gone that is about as real as aliens in space. So what do you do? Still go mad most likely, if we're honest. And a fair share of the Lost do. The suicide rate among us is quite high actually. Others drop out after a couple of decades or centuries because they can't take it anymore and more often than not end up running businesses in spaceports to avoid "real" society. The rest of us? We find a way to cope. Ally for example, a person who thrives off of human interaction and contact – I asked her once why she became part of the Lost and she got mad and didn't talk with me for three whole tours, so I dropped it – hits each and every bar, tavern and whorehouse she can find, stocking up on physical contact with other human beings. I suspect she is far more lonely than she lets on, and over the years, she has found her own way of connecting with people, brief as it may be.

Haru is big into languages. She is fluent in ten of them and she is always delighted to find out about how structure, words and overall application have changed over time and why. She uses shore leave primarily to stock up on new material and to freshen up her knowledge. I guess it is her way to stay in touch with humanity. The Captain is big on books. Her whole cabin is full of them, and by now, a fair share of paperbacks have spilled over into the common room. None of us dares to call her out on that, because you know, her ship and such, but let me put it like this: The Captain has been the captain of the Dolos for almost six hundred years. Imagine the amount of books amassed over that time period. Marlon suggested once she should get rid of a couple and she nearly tossed him out the airlock. Touchy subject that. And speaking of the devil: I don't know, and neither do I give a fuck, about what Marlon does during shore leave. I make it a habit to see that asshole as little as possible. Me? Well, I am big into visual media. Movies, series, games, holo-vids, you name it. The upside of being asleep for decades at a time is that you amass a backlog of material. It is also a very easy hobby to maintain. Every shore leave I purchase and download new material onto my pad and that is it. No paperbacks spilling into the common room for me, no sir! It also helps with being a Preemie. These first couple of days that you spend mostly lying around and feeling sorry for yourself as the cryo drugs wash out of your system are made indefinitely less horrible by focusing on a show that you can binge a couple seasons of, while thawing up. Other than that, I don't really interact with people much. As I said, the whole theme park mentality of the spaceports tends to annoy me. Luckily, as Chief Engineer, I have to spend at least part of my shore leave on board the Dolos anyways, supervising repairs and such. But it's okay. I like to be alone. The weird ambivalence of being alone while having a place in this tight-knit group – a family – on board the Dolos is what feels like home to me. I know every square inch of this ruddy, old ship. Probably fixed and/or exchanged it at least once too! The Dolos is an unwieldy abomination of a spacecraft, shaped somewhere between a brick and a bloated stingray, but it is my abomination. This ugly old junkheap of a ship is my favorite place in the Verse. The Captain is our mom, Haru and Ally are the two sisters I never had, the nerdy and the slutty one. And Marlon is the weird asshole of an uncle nobody can stand and who yells racial slurs on Thanksgiving. To be completely honest though, Marlon gets along with the others just fine, so maybe it is just something between the two of us. I've never been great with alpha male types. And it is not like we openly antagonise each other – well most of the time. He just gets under my skin, and I probably annoy him equally, but we make do, because that is what you do in a family. You stick with each other even if you drive each other nuts. I heard a saying once: "Family is a four-letter-word!" Very funny. Had a good laugh at that one. So when the Captain sent word that we're about to go on the next tour, naturally I was the first one to report back to the Dolos, all decked out with a renewed hatred for all things society and a couple of terabytes full of new media material, ready to go "back home". Within a couple of hours the whole crew was back and getting busy with cataloging and categorizing the cargo – apart from Ally who, as usual, had fucked off to the med bay with the pretext of taking inventory of the medical supplies (read as: sleeping off one hell of a hangover and maybe taking medication for STIs). The Captain had worked her magic and somehow managed to fill the Dolos up to the brim with cargo, despite Dionysus being a slow port. She had scooped up every shipment that had been waiting for ages to get off Dionysus. It meant that our next tour would take us almost the whole way across the galaxy, but we would most likely turn a profit on that trip.

Among the cargo was the usual – building prefabs and medical supplies that were always needed, especially on outer rim colonies – as well as one bigger container that came with a sizable blind-fee, meaning we didn't know what was in it and were paid twice for the privilege of not opening the container during transit. That specific container shipment had come in only the day before and had finally maxed out the cargo hold of the Dolos. Once everything was catalogued and the pre-launch checklist was checked over (twice, once by the XO, once by the Captain), the whole crew got together in the common room for the usual briefing. It is one of my favorite things to do if I am honest, almost like a family tradition. Everyone brings something to eat from the spaceport, and we sit together and go over what happened during shore leave, what we have loaded and anything else that needs discussing. It is one of the few times where we get everyone together and not all conversation is based on work.

I was poking unenthusiastically at a box of some kind of fusion food – I believe it was Indian-Croatian – listening only half-heartedly to Ally, who was just telling the rest of the crew about her latest sexual conquests in such excruciating detail that it made even Marlon blush, when the Captain introduced us to our tourist for this trip. The Dolos usually didn't take on tourists, but we have a spare cryo pod for emergencies, and the guy offered, to quote the Captain, "a shit ton of money" for passage. Since the profit margin for this trip was shallow enough, she was eager to take the opportunity. The crew half-heartedly agreed and "welcomed" Dwight with a couple of mumbled words at the end of the briefing. Two hours before we went into cryostasis, the Dolos undocked from Dionysus Port and slowly cleared orbit.

CHAPTER III

Waking up from cryo isn't exactly like waking up in bed. You don't dream in cryo, but when you decant, you have some notion that time has passed. I know that since I crawled into this pod, more time has passed than I subjectively remember – it is just hard to understand it consciously.

That feeling of time gone by is always the first thing that hits me coming out of cryo. In that blissful moment where your brain is not yet aware that your body has been immobile and frozen for thirty years and is aching like a motherfucker, your thoughts are faster than any FTL drive. I wade through unfiltered impressions and emotions and try to piece together some sort of coherent thought. Right next to a feeling of annoyance and the face of my XO, I find the fact that I am in my cryo pod. I take the second turn to the left from a cozy feeling of genuine affection towards Haru and remember that we've been under for the better part of thirty years. And at the crossing between memories of my favorite pre-space era TV show and a fond remembrance of all the bullshit Ally and I like to talk, framed right next to a memory of a match shorter than all the other matches, I remember that I am the designated Preemie for this run.

The realization hits around the same time as the pain. My nervous system has finally thawed up enough to remember how to process stimuli, and right now it is processing two things: A: "It is damn fucking cold in here" B: "Holy shit, everything hurts." I immediately start to shiver uncontrollably. With a motion that has more in common with a muscle spasm than a coordinated movement, I slam my fist against the pod release and flinch at the sharp noise of the pod sliding open. A white hot ten inch nail is pressing itself between the hemispheres of my brain, and my whole body is covered in pinpricks as it slowly starts to circulate blood again. I open my eyes and resist the urge to close them against the cold fluorescent light of the cryo bay and the stinging sensation that is slowly covering the surface of my eyeballs. I squint and focus on the door to cryo prep, and with another clumsy spasm movement, I set myself adrift towards it. Thank god for zero-G. This would be a lot more of a nightmare if I had to deal with gravity at this point. But like all the other systems, artificial gravity is on spring break right now. I've overestimated the duration of my short zero-G travel though and bang against the cryo prep door with more force than I intended to. I barely manage to curl up before the cold steel hits my shoulder. Another flavor of pain added to this glorious experience. I'd scream and curse if my throat wasn't already on fire and my lungs wouldn't be at max capacity with just processing the stale air. So I settle for a very masculine whimper and murderous thoughts. I fight the urge to throw up. Doing that in zero-G is a bad idea. Somehow, I grab hold of a handle next to the door, and with another jerk of my free hand, I hit the control panel to start the Preemie routine. Barely remembering to brace myself before artificial gravity takes effect, I stand there, my whole body shaking uncontrollably, still holding on to the handle like it is my mom's hand on the first day of school. I stop resisting the urge any longer and throw up. Somewhere in my pain ravaged brain, I spend half a thought on having to clean that up later, but find that I cannot even pretend to care right now. I hear the trademark hiss of life support coming online, and the room becomes brighter as the ship switches from emergency lighting to full illumination. I stand there, me and my handhold, hating it. After what feels like an eternity, the door to cryo prep slides open. I shuffle around the newly created puddle of bodily fluids, managing to both not step into it and not fall on my face doing so, and am greeted with another hiss from the Preemie locker, as the ship repressurises it before springing open the locker. The sight of Ally's Preemie cocktail nearly makes me cream my pants, and after another minute of uncoordinated fumbling around, I even manage to administer it. I reach into the locker for a vacuum sealed plastic package and pull it out. With the stubborn effort of a man who knows he has the worst almost behind him, I tear off the plastic wrap and unfold a thermal blanket, almost instantly crashing down on the Preemie-bed, the bare bones cot located next to the Preemie locker.

Ally's cocktail gets to work and is starting to dull the various aches in my body. God bless her. I really need to buy her a pint or two next time we dock. My body taken over by a beautiful haze of drugs, I fall asleep. I wake up almost thirty-six hours later. The effects of the Preemie decanting have decreased to a state that lets me get up and, wrapped snugly in my termo blanket, shuffle gingerly from the cryo prep room to the common room to make some coffee. Naturally, Ally's cocktail now adds a marvelous drug induced hangover to the overall soreness of cryo decanting. Life is fun. Over my comatose thirty-six hour sleeping marathon, both my body and the Dolos have become significantly more habitable. Reactivated full life support has not only pumped in fresh air, but also dialed up the heating (you know, space is cold). I still shiver under my blanket, but no longer because of the cold around me. I take solace in the fact that the worst is over as I half sit, half slump next to the coffee machine as I wait for the black elixir of the gods to run through the filter. Smelling freshly brewed coffee is one of those things I will never tire off. I wrap myself tighter in my blanket, and despite my hangover and overall misery, I find myself smiling. You see, I bitch a lot about being Preemie, but to be completely honest, once the whole waking up to a world of pain and misery part is over, I quite enjoy it. The next week I will spend by myself, which is a rare luxury working on a LSCT freighter. You are constantly around your shipmates, and spaceports are always crowded with all kinds of folk. I always was a person that needed some alone time every now and again to fill up the old social batteries. Sure, my shipmates are like family to me, but the thought of binging some show on my tablet for the next week or so while the rest of the crew slowly decants... there are worse things in life. With a mug of steaming hot coffee in my hand, I shuffle back to cryo and look at my shipmates in their tubes. I know it is kinda creepy but watching them sleep helps me realize that I am in fact not as alone as it appears. While I like to be alone, feeling alone is no fun. Weird how the human brain works, right? There is more than one story floating around of Preemies going stir crazy in the endless vacuum of space. If you ever think of your ship as a metal box floating through an endless void, you have no other option apart from losing it. I mean, it is the reasonable thing to do. Space travel is insane if you think about it too hard. So if it means I have to play the creepy uncle every once in a while to avoid that, that's fine with me.

Ready to initiate the weeklong slow decanting for the rest of the crew, I step towards the cryo console. I start with a regular systems check for both the cryo systems and the Dolos' overall systems. If something broke during transit I would need to at least try and fix it before they woke up or the Captain would chew me out. All looks fine, which is a pleasant surprise. Given the fact that we were en route for almost thirty years I expected to have to do at least SOME maintenance. Well, I am not one to complain about less work, so I bring up the program to initiate the decanting of the crew.

"Rise and shine boys and girls," I croak. my voice still not up to par after decanting, and hit execute. A red warning flashes on the screen. "What the fuck?"

Are you sure you want to initiate decant_crew_guided.exe? The estimated rest transit time exceeds the duration of decant_crew_guided.exe by more than 3000 %. I look at the words but it takes my brain some time to process their meaning. My mouth opens and closes a couple of times as I am trying to make sense of that message. I put the coffee mug down and interface with the Dolos' main control. I am not much of a navigator but I know a bit of how to determine the ship's place in space if I have to. One of the, if not THE ONLY useful contribution to the crew XO Dickhead has added was to make sure everyone had a crash course in the Dolos' operating system in case they needed to check things outside their speciality on Preemie duty. Begrudgingly I have to admit, he had a point. I determine our current position as well as our journey's goal and calculate the differences. I don't like the result so I calculate it twice more in case my hungover brain has made a mistake. It hasn't. We're still ten years out. "Why the fuck did you wake me then?" I mumble to myself not really expecting the Dolos to answer.

I check the cryo systems for malfunctions. Nothing. I use the ship's main diagnostics to check the cryo system externally for malfunctions. Nothing. It wasn't a misfiring of the cryo system then.

I open the direct query-based interface to the AI that runs the Dolos' main systems. AI makes it sound smart if we're honest. It is more a never ending if/else construct that reacts to certain situations in a non-creative way. But since this sentence doesn't make sense – even to me – we call it AI and everyone knows you're talking about the ship's governing system. A glorified chatbot, fed with all of the ship's sensory information. The query-based interface lets you "talk" to it, and if you are using simple enough words, you might even get an answer. The art of "talking" to the AI is to figure out which words you need to use to get the output you need. More out of spite than out of any rational thought I start with,

"Why did you wake me?"

Query cannot be processed. Please rephrase …

Well, it was worth a shot.

"Status report of crew."

Crew in Cryo - 4 of 5.

Crew decanted - 1 of 5.

"You're right so far!"

Query cannot be processed. Please rephrase …

I really need to stop sassing a computer program.

"Specify normal timeframe for decant_crew_preemie.exe in relation to journey completion."

Journey completion minus [168] hours.

"Specify journey_completion_current."

Journey completion in [9] Y - [360] D - [18] H - [53] M.

"Specify last execution of decant_crew_preemie.exe"

Last execution of decant_crew_preemie.exe [1] D - [15] H - [32] M ago.

"Specify difference between the timeframe from last execution of decant_crew_preemie.exe in relation to journey completion and the established norm"

Irregular.

"Yeah, no shit!" Okay, at least the system hasn't bugged out or something. The internal chronometer seems to work.

"Access system logs."

System logs accessed. Choose category…

"Executables - Details."

Category accessed. Formulate query…

"Full entry decant_crew_preemie.exe."

The screen fills with all entries of when Preemies were decanted. I tap on the last entry – my rude early Preemie awakening not even two days ago. The system shows me all the standard data. Who was the Preemie, when was the program executed, did it complete successfully etc. I am merely interested in the "Trigger" section. Normally, when you awake, as you are supposed to, seven days before the Dolos reaches its destination, the "Trigger" section reads something along the line of "planned, automated execution" or something like that. This time however I was looking at an entirely different "Trigger". Whoever programmed the system apparently didn't think that this trigger message would be visible to any non-tech personnel, because it is filled with technical wooblidoo and I am barely able to understand what the fuck it means. Reading through it multiple times I think my decanting was triggered because there was some sort of unscheduled activity in the cryo system, which, to be fair, would make sense. IF there was a mishap with cryo you'd want someone to take a look at it and not wake up decades later to realize half your crew has turned into permanent popsicles. What doesn't make sense is that, as I already established, there was no malfunction in the cryo system. I look up at my shipmates.

"Now who of you fucks got up late to get a glass of warm milk, huh?" I look between the four of them in their cosy cryo pods. Wait… my hungover brain screams at me that something is off, but my conscious thought struggles to nail it down. All four of them accounted for. Haru, Ally, the Captain and XO Dickhead. What am I missing? It hits me like a ton of bricks and my head snaps to the now empty pod of our tourist. Adrenalin floods my system, and all of a sudden, my hangover nearly vanishes. I am not the only one awake.

CHAPTER IV

I feel guilty as I walk from shipmate to shipmate and pour coffee into their mugs, which they raised at me trembling as they all go through a Preemie hangover. They sit in the middle of the common room like a bundle of misery.

At first, I had only woken up the Captain to explain the situation, but she quickly decided we had to deal with this as a crew, as a family. So we did, resulting in a very, very cryo sick crew.

The Captain is putting on a brave face for the rest, but she is still in the thick of it herself, wrapped in a thermal blanket, doing her best not to shudder, her lower lip betraying her effort. As the only fully functioning shipmate, I do what I can with blankets and coffee and ibuprofen. I empty the last of the coffee into Haru's mug and add a shitton of sugar and cream to it, just as she likes it, when the Captain decides to disrupt the sea of moans, groans and nervous shuffling from her crew.

"As you might have guessed, we have a situation on board", her voice still hoarse from cryo, but solid, firm, something to rely on. XO Marlon, Haru and I turn our gaze to the Captain. Ally cocks her head in acknowledgement, her eyes still closed, not willing to expand her world past her eyelids for the fear of the cryo hangover spilling out and gaining more ground. "We're not going to dock within a week, in fact, we're roughly ten years out," the Captain starts.

"Why are we awake then?" Marlon drawls even thicker than usual, his tongue still drowsy by the cryo hangover. The Captain nods to me so I pick up where she left off.

"Once I managed to get past the Preemie hangover, I realized the computer woke me early," I start, keeping my voice low as to not further torture anybody in the room. "The system initiated my Preemie routine because of an unscheduled cryo activity. At least that is all I can figure out by myself from the log entry." I take a deep breath before I continue. "It looks like this unscheduled cryo activity was the decanting of our tourist, who incidentally hasn't been found on the ship so far."

Marlon looks at me with a puzzled expression. "That is weird and all, but why are we all awake for that?" "Because he woke me," the Captain takes back over, her voice carrying a tone that shuts down all further questions regarding the matter, even from XO Dickhead. "As is protocol in such a situation by the way. And I told him to wake the rest of the crew." She takes a sip of her coffee, savoring the warmth as it runs down her throat.

"This tourist can be anywhere on the ship and I don't want people to go looking for him by themselves. We don't know who he is, what he is capable of and what agenda he is after." She stands up and sheds the termo blanket.

"Steve, I want you to check the cryo log and figure out when and why that "unscheduled cryo activity" happened. Haruto, I want you to check if we're still on course, or if anything has been tampered with. Ally you do the same for communication systems and check if anything was sent to or from the Dolos while we were out. Kevin, you know the crawlspaces and nooks and crannies of the Dolos the best, so the two of us, we're going on a search for our tourist." Everyone nods in agreement.

"Ally, can you mix us a Preemie cocktail, like you did for Ottenberg?" the XO croaks as he gets up and has to steady himself on the wall. Ally finally opens her eyes at that. She looks a bit sheepish. "Sorry Steve, but if I mix that cocktail for all of us now, we're completely out of pain meds, and we're still ten years out." "I don't want that, especially if we still have an unknown factor running awol on the ship," the Captain chimes in.

"Well lucky for Ottenberg I guess," Marlon snarls and shuffles towards the cryo room. I watch him leave and have to fight very hard not to retort in a mean way.

"There is loads to do people. Let's get it done. The sooner we have the tourist back in his pod, the sooner everyone gets to take a nap again!" The Captain brings me out of my head back into the room. "I want everyone to meet back up here in four hours with results!" The rest of us start to get busy. There is a lot of moaning and shuffling, but there is action.

The Captain comes over to me. "So ideas how to start this?" "Well, I already sealed off the living quarters of the Dolos before I woke you guys. I am not keen on getting backstabbed, so the bridge, the crew quarters, the common room and the cryo facilities are all clean. These are the parts of the ship that I can actually scan for life signs." She nods focusing her gaze on a stray paperback lying next to us on the floor while she thinks it through. "So he is definitely somewhere in the cargo hold, or the engine room." "Or one of the crawl spaces in between them," I add with an unvoiced "sorry" on my face. "Can you close down all crawl spaces remotely?" "Once we're at the central cargo hub, yes. From there, I can also check if there are any cargo containers that have been accessed, opened, you know, the works." She nods, again thinking it over. Ships like the Dolos are built modular, meaning the main component of the ship that houses the bridge, the cryo pods, the common room and so on is manufactured by itself. The cargo part with all its subsystems is built by another company. Since most ship captains are cheap, the two components have a minimum of cross wiring and stay mostly autonomously. Can't really blame the Captain though, our situation right now isn't exactly common.

"Alright, go talk to Steve if we can borrow his baseball bat from his cabin. I think we still have a motion sensor somewhere on the bridge. We seal the common area behind us and work our way to the cargo hub. Then we take it piece by piece until we find the guy." "Sounds like a plan Captain!" She shuffles off towards the bridge while I begrudgingly go back to cryo. Talking to the XO, my favorite pastime. I find the red-faced Texan sitting on the floor in the cryo room, in front of the cryo console he has clipped out of its stand and laid on the floor in front of him. He's still wrapped in a blanket and hugging his coffee mug. The big man from the big state doesn't seem all that imposing and alpha to me as he usually does. He doesn't look up when I enter the cryo chamber.

"What you want?" he drawls underneath his breath while continuing to access the system in front of him.

"Captain asked if we can borrow your baseball bat?"

At that, he looks up at me with a dumbfounded expression. He starts to form the words "what for" but then I can see his thoughts catching on.

"Good idea. It is under the cot in my bunk," he slurs, focusing back on the system, the conversation over.

I step closer and get the feeling that he tenses up.

"Found anything yet?" "The fuck you want Ottenberg? Smalltalk? Really?" I suck in a breath and release it slowly and audibly through my mouth, suppressing an urge to kick him.

"Can we play nice for a change? I'm somewhat freaking out and I am curious as to if you already found something." See, that wasn't half bad. It almost sounded genuine. "Shit, sorry man!" Marlon rubs at his eyes. Did the XO just really use the word "sorry"? "You know better than anyone what a bitch this cryo hangover is. I am cranky, that's all."

He takes a couple of deep breaths and looks at me.

"All I can say so far is that there was some sort of patch uploaded to the system before we took off. Which is weird, because we a) didn't request one, and b) it didn't raise any flags when it patched the system. That is some piece of code that is a lot smarter than me, if I am completely honest. Fucked over the log and the protocols mighty fine." Marlon looks back at the screen with the look of someone who is ready to admit defeat.

"Guess I have to go through the backend code line by line and see where shit was added before I can check what's what." "But you'll be able to access the logs eventually?" I ask, trying my hardest to not sound as tense as I am.

"Might be, might not be. Hard to say with invasive shit like this. I don't want to fuck around too much, we still want to be able to go back to sleep eventually, right?" "I can do without a ten year space trip for sure. Thanks Marlon. I leave you to it!" The XO raises a hand at me in a gesture that is more a "get lost" than a "farewell", and I leave him with an uneasy feeling. It is time to hunt a tourist.

CHAPTER V

With a mechanical hiss the sealed door to the cargo hold opens and both the Captain and I are immediately hit by cold, stale air. This area of the Dolos technically holds atmosphere, but life support only warms it up enough so our lungs won't freeze. That's why we're both wrapped in several layers of clothing, the Captain in at least two sweaters underneath her old military jacket and myself with a couple of shirts, a hoodie and a thick thermo jacket. With our winter hats and thick gloves, we look like a couple of kindergarten kids whose overprotective mothers prepared them for their first snow outing. We take a step into the cargo hold and I tighten my grip around XO Dickhead's baseball bat. The Captain does a sweep in front of us with an ancient looking motion sensor before she turns to the control panel next to the door behind us and reseals it. We're officially on our own now. "Why do I feel like Sigourney Weaver with this thing?" she waves the motion sensor overly dramatic and grins at me. The smile feels awkward and forced. I can't blame her. Neither of us is in the mood for this. We make our way to the central cargo hub without any activity on the motion sensor.

"Are you sure this thing is working Captain? I mean, that thing is nearly as old as you!" I tease her to fill the awkward silence between us.
"Careful Kevin! We wouldn't want you to "accidentally" fall out of an airlock, now would we?" We both chuckle. She does a 360 degree sweep around the central cargo hub terminal and gives me a nod. I step up to the terminal and wake up the screen. "Shit!" "What is it?" The Captain keeps her eyes trained on the various dark hallways that meet at the central hub and go out to the individual cargo containers. "Someone used the console." "Our tourist?" "Unless one of the crew did a little sleepwalk, who else?" I shoot back a bit sharper than I intended. An awkward pause. "Sorry Captain, this whole situation ..." "Nevermind Kevin. Can you check what was accessed?" A sad smile creeps onto my face. Bless her heart, she is trying her best to keep this ship and its crew afloat. "Give me a second." I work my magic and bring up the interaction protocol. "He accessed the shipping manifest." I scroll through the protocol and jam my finger on a specific entry. "There. A34/0320."
The Captain turns around to locate the hallway that will lead us to that cargo entry.
"What was in that one?" "Medical supplies." I tell the system to highlight the way to that specific cargo entry, and a string of blue guiding lights come to life up on the ceiling, leading us down one of the hallways. I pick up the baseball bat again and force myself to take a deep breath of cold, stale air. We follow the guiding lights down the hallway, cargo containers to our left and right. Twice we come to a crossing, and twice we take a turn to the left. The Captain's eyes are painfully trained on the display of the motion tracker. Thankfully, it stays silent. I check the numbers on the containers passing us by: A34/0310, A34/0311 – we're getting closer. We walk past a brand new looking container in a metallic looking dark grey. I whistle through my teeth.

"That thing looks fancy!" "It should be for the price they paid us to ship it blindy."
I look the container over as we pass it. Most cargo containers have been in use for several centuries and look the part. It is rare to see something new and shiny like this. I wonder what material it is made out of. "There it is!" The Captain snaps me out of my thoughts. "A34/0320. And wouldn't you know it, someone has tampered with it." I follow her gaze to a far more usual container, painted in a red that makes it hard to tell where the paint starts and the rust begins. One of the access doors has been forced open. We nod at each other and take position. The Captain on the right side of the door, reaching for the handle in order to open it towards her. Me on the left side, raising the baseball bat, my heart in my throat, determined to force its way out of my body. We look at each other and the Captain forms a voiceless "Three, two, one..." before she janks open the container door and I rush in, ready for violence. Instead of a masculine display of combat however, my foot brushes against something mushy, gets caught in it, and I tumble onto the container floor alongside the baseball bat. The container is filled with the sound of my body and the bat making friends with the metal floor, followed by a respectable string of profanities. "Shit Kevin, you should charge money for that." The Captain laughs and activates the light in the container.
"Are you hurt?" "Only my ego"
She helps me up. As I reach for the baseball bat, we both suddenly stop moving. The Captain's eyes widen in shock and a barely audible gasp escapes her mouth. There is an almost frozen body on the floor. We found our tourist.

CHAPTER VI

"Yep, that is our tourist", the Captain raises up from inspecting the body. Her face set in hard lines. "Shot several times in the chest, probably by that gun" She points to a cheap looking gun lying not far from the body. "Probably?" I look at her, raising my eyebrows. "As far as I am aware, there are no guns on this ship. Isn't that like one of your biggest rules?" "Does any of this look like it is in any way sanctioned by me?" she snaps at me. She struggles to maintain the cool, collected aura of a captain in command. "Fuck Kevin, I don't know. All of this is so fucked up!" She helplessly runs her hands through her hair. We both look at the body. None of us wants to address the obvious. Either we have a stowaway on board, or whoever murdered our tourist here is one of the crew. The first one means there is someone on the ship who is committed enough to sacrifice thirty years of their existence and is capable of murder, because I sure as shit didn't see anyone apart from Mr Popsickle here and the crew in the cryo chamber. The second option I don't even want to think about. The Captain pulls out her handheld from underneath her jacket and snaps a couple of quick pictures of the container, the victim and the gun. Less than half an hour later, we step out of the cargo hold and back into the main ship.

"Seal the cargo hold again." The Captain looks at me. It feels like she's aged several years on our way back from the crime scene. "And make sure to disable the control panel on the other side." She averts her eyes. "If we have a stowaway on board, I don't want him anywhere near the crew." She steps over to the intercom.

"Everybody, meeting in the common room in five!"

I watch her leave. The burden she is carrying is almost visible. I feel a pang of guilt. I should have helped her more. For the second time in less than twelve hours, the smell of coffee fills the common room. I am tempted to close my eyes and pretend that none of this is happening, savoring the smell of the warm cup of coffee in my hands, letting it drag me back to that blissful moment when I waited for the coffee to run through the filter right after I slept off the worst of the Premie hangover. But it's no use. Time to face the music.

The whole crew sits around the table, grabbing their coffee mugs as if they were the only thing to give them support. Everyone's a bit wide eyed and on edge. The Captain is about to drop a nuke on them.

"Our tourist is dead," she puts it bluntly and pauses to give her words time to soak in. I study my shipmates. Haru's jaw drops in shock, her eyes finding me, asking unvoiced questions. I try to give her a reassuring smile, but find that I am all out of reassuring. Marlon's eyes narrow at the news, but his face remains calm. As usual, I can't really read him. Ally just looks at the Captain with an expression that seems to wait for the punchline of a particularly nasty joke. Once that punchline does not come, she seems a bit sheepish and looks around the room in an unsure, very un-Ally-like way. Odd. "He was shot multiple times in the chest by a gun we found next to him." The Captain takes a deep breath. "Now is the time any of you can come

forward to tell me you smuggled a gun onto the Dolos. I won't be mad. We just need all the information possible."
Silence. "Steve?" The Captain shoots a questioning look at the XO.
"Hey don't look at me Maria" Marlon raises his hands in defense. "I got rid of my gun on Dionysus, just like you asked me to." "You have a gun on board?" Haru beats me to it. "HAD. It was stupid. Maria found it, chewed me out and made me get rid of it." The XO crosses his arms in front of his barrelchest. "It is gone now. Whatever gun killed that poor bastard, it wasn't mine." "And we're supposed to believe that a big badass Texan like you only owns ONE gun!" I find myself getting really angry. I am not sure if I actually like to think the XO could have killed the tourist, or if I just feel annoyed that the Captain didn't kick him off the ship for this violation of trust. "Frankly I don't give a shit what you think Ottenberg! I am loyal to Maria. To the Captain. If she believes me, that is good enough for me." "Oh, and the fact that you endangered the entire crew over and over again is supposed to…"
"ENOUGH!" the Captain's roar silences the both of us as it cuts through the common room. Haru flinches. More at the ugly edge of the Captain's voice than the volume. "Until we are not entirely sure what happened we will NOT jump to ANY conclusions!"
Both the XO and I study our feet. I feel a rush of warmth in my face as it starts to redden, both in anger and shame. "If Steve says he has no gun on board, I believe him."
I start to voice my objection but the Captain shuts me up with an unquestionable stare.
"Which means we have to consider that the tourist stowed the weapon on board without us noticing, OR even worse, we have a stowaway on board." Again, the Captain paused to let her words run their course in the minds of her crew. "What else do we know?" "There was a minor course alteration towards the outer rim of the sector shortly before we decanted," Haru started.

"Alongside a minor encoded transmission towards that outer rim around the same time," Ally picked up where Haru left off.

"Haru and I cross referenced, and it seems that the destination of our flightpath as well as the destination of the signal are the same." "Okay, that is something." The Captain said, happy for a lead – any lead really. " I take it you corrected the course again?"

Haru nodded. "What about cryo?" the Captain looked at the XO, who took a deep breath before he started talking. "It is a mess. All I know for now is that there was some sort of rogue process which piggybacked along the Preemie wake-up routine." "Wait! Piggybacked?" Ally looks at him not entirely sure she understands what he is saying. "So the tourist woke up AFTER Kevin?" The XO nods and looks at me cooly. "I don't have access to the protocols yet, but yes, it is technically not possible for him to have woken up before you Ottenberg."

Everyone looks at me now. I swallow the urge to get into XO Dickhead's face for not giving me a heads up first. Basically setting me up.

"What time frame are we talking? Ally's cocktail knocked me out for at least twelve hours." Now it is my turn to throw my hands up in defense. "The fucking ship could have exploded and gone tits up and I wouldn't have noticed!" "Well isn't that convenient for you," the XO snarls. "You got something to say Marlon?" I rise up, all good intentions thrown out the window. I fucking hate that prick.

"Both of you shut the fuck up, or I'll throw the two of you out of the airlock!" The Captain has enough of our shit. The XO shoots her a look that almost looks apologetic. That is off brand for him. "I don't want to hear another word from either of you unless it adds to FIXING this situation. Am I understood?" "Yes ma'am," both of us sheepishly mumble. "Alright Steve, I want you to keep working on those protocols. Might help us establish a

timeline. Also, Kevin, take a piece of paper and write down what you remember since you decanted. Try to figure out the timestamps as precisely as possible."
Both of us nod.
"Haruto, you go over the database and see if you can find anything about the criminal elements in this sector. If this is some weirdass pirate stunt, I want to know who we're dealing with. And Ally, the container we found the tourist in was filled with medical supplies. I want you to go over the contents and tell me if there is anything in it that could fetch a nice price off the record." At the mention of the medical supplies, I think I see Ally tense up. Before I can put my finger on it though, she catches herself and is already nodding again. "I know this is stressful but if we keep a cool head, we can get through this." The Captain focussed our attention back on her. "No one goes into the cargo hold without my permission. You all have your tasks, go work on them!" With a couple of unsure glances, the crew starts moving again.

CHAPTER VII

When Haru enters my cabin an hour after the all-hands meeting, she finds me sitting on my cot, a piece of paper in hand. She closes the door behind her.

"You okay?"

I try to smile at her, but falter halfway through. "Not really no. I have roughly twenty-four to thirty-six hours of passed-out-ness in my schedule and, I don't know, something tells me XO gunslinger won't be happy with that." I try to throw the piece of paper melodramatically on the small table next to my cot. Defiant, the paper sheet floats slowly past it and onto the floor as if it is trying to mock me. "I am fucked Haru!" I slump my shoulders and stare sullenly onto the floor. "Even I wouldn't believe me that I had nothing to do with the tourist's murder, looking at that time sheet!" I shudder at how blankly I can put it. Haru sits down next to me and puts her arms around me. She doesn't say anything. For a woman who knows so much about language and words, she has an unmatched ability to know when to stay silent. I close my eyes and drink in the feeling of her touch. The warmth of her body next to mine, the faint smell of vanilla from her perfume.

We sit in silence for what seems like forever.

"I don't think you're involved in this," she finally breaks the silence, her voice barely a whisper. "I don't think any of the crew is for that matter."

I shoot her a questionable glance. She looks at me with mock annoyance.

"Yes I know, you don't like Steve, but do you honestly think he could kill someone?" "Well his ego is big enough to smash someone's skull in!" We both chuckle at that. Haru rests her head on my shoulder. "Thank you for this Haru!" "What?" "For saying it out loud. I needed to hear that." I pull her into an embrace and kiss her. We let ourselves fall back onto my cot, and one thing leads to another. Yes... Haru and me, we are dating. In secret. Which is quite the feat on a ship where privacy doesn't really exist. Not to speak of the Captain's rule of no fraternisation. I try not to think of the fact that this relationship is probably coming to an end soon. It is only a matter of time until XO Dickhead restores the cryo protocols and figures out that for the last ten trips or so, every time I was Preemie, Haru was decanted shortly after me. It was a little more than bad luck why I was selected for Preemie duty. XO Dickhead always put the short straw all the way to the left. We would steal these weeks away for the two of us. A couple of days at a time, just me and her. Our little secret. Sure we'd hook up occasionally while docked at a port, but you always had to be careful that the rest of the crew didn't find out. And between me having to coordinate repairs and her stocking up on navigational information and merging conflicting star charts, we had little time anyways. We were always distracted with something else, outstanding tasks we had to take care of, or the fear that we'd be discovered. None of that mattered during our post-cryo dates. Just the two of us, an empty ship and the vastness of space. Honestly I wasn't aware of how lonely I'd become until Haru and I started this whole thing. The human mind has a way of tricking itself and rationalizing all your personal issues. I told myself I didn't like people, I liked to be alone, I didn't need anyone. If I felt the urge for something physical, I could always visit a whorehouse while docked at port. And while all of these things are somewhat true, over time they built up a harsh emotional pressure and made me miserable. That misery shaped me into a bitter and self-loathing man. Once I realized there was someone who cared about me, that misery was taken off me like a blindfold. It is not just butterflies and kisses and sex; in a true partnership, and excuse me for thinking Haru and I have something like that, you share your thoughts, your happiness, and yes, also your misery. The short moment she'd spent on hugging me and voicing her faith in me cost her nothing and meant everything to me. It's funny how the smallest gestures, whether intended or not, can have a huge impact on the people around you, isn't it? So I lose myself in her embrace, and for a short moment, all my worries and fears are far away. There is no dead tourist, there is no accusing XO, there is no compromising cryo protocol. There is only this wonderful woman. She is me and I am her. There is us, and there is the rest of the galaxy. Like all good things in the world though, this moment of bliss does come to an end. Specifically to a loud, obnoxious, Texan end.

Haru and I are lying on my cot, enjoying the afterglow. My blanket spread halfheartedly over our naked bodies. BAM! BAM! – "Ottenberg? You in there? We need to talk!" XO Dickhead is banging against my cabin door. Shit! Haru and I look at each other, terrified. I jump up from the cot and gesture wildly toward my closet.

"Go hide in there!" I whisper while frantically wrapping my bed sheet around my waist.

"Ottenberg? The fuck are you doing in there? I can hear you. Open the goddamn door!" I panic, run to the shower cell, turn on the water, put my head under it, panik some more, check if Haru managed to get into the tiny closet and finally, taking a deep breath, open the cabin door.

"The fuck you naked for?" XO Dickhead drawls and shoves himself past me into the cabin without asking.

"Oh please, by all means, come in!" I close the door behind him, annoyance slowly surpassing terror. "I was about to take shower so if you've come to hurl more accusations my way, can you wait? Preferably forever?"

"Cute! Aren't you supposed to compile a timeline of your," and Marlon puts it in air quotes, "Preemie duties?" Have I mentioned that I hate this man? Marlon is looking around my cabin suspiciously. I point towards the sheet of paper on the floor, hoping to draw his gaze away from the closet.

"That is as far as I can get it nailed down. I was hoping a shower would help me clear my head and get some more detail" I force my face into the fakest, most shit-eatingest of all grins. "To not further inconvenience you." He lets a mocking chuckle slip and picks up the piece of paper. "Oh Ottenberg, you're in trouble. A day and a half of drug induced comatose sleep." He lets the paper fall back down and looks at me with a vicious grin. "I am afraid that won't do! So I hope that magical shower of yours does the trick!" He glances at the bedsheet around my waist and then to the closet. I try my hardest not to flinch. "Say Ottenberg, you always dry off using a bed sheet?"

His grin takes on a predatory nature as he slowly walks to the closet. "Let me get a towel for you!" I try to interfere but he has already opened the closet and is looking at Haru, who is trying to cover her naked body with a shirt of mine she pulled off the hanger. Marlon lets out a whistle through his teeth, and his face turns back to me, still grinning. "Well I be damned Ottenberg. Always thought you were one of them queer folk!" He holds out a hand to Haru and helps her out of the closet, never taking his eyes off of me. "I gotta say Ottenberg. That is some premium piece of ass you've caught yourself there!" I know he is baiting me, provoking a reaction. But the caveman part of my brain simply doesn't care. I charge at him. Trying to get between him and Haru. My woman. Ugga Ugga. Kevin big club. Kevin alpha caveman... I blame this questionable decision on post coital hormones. Obviously Marlon is an asshole. But he isn't an idiot, and he is far more comfortable with all this caveman shit than I am. He probably knew I was going to take a swing at him long before I did, and he is ready for it.

He sidesteps me, and my momentum drags me past him. When I turn around, all I can do is look angrily at his fist as it crashes down onto my face. With a sickening crack, I feel my nose break, and my world explodes into searing pain, snot and blood. Somewhere far away, I hear Haru scream and tell Marlon to stop, but all I can rationally compute at this point is that my nose really fucking hurts, and what is this, oh, apparently I am lying on the floor butt-naked as my bed sheet has disappeared between me storming at Marlon and me getting punched out like a lightweight. Hey, if you are going to do this caveman shit, you might as well dress for it, right? "Don't get too comfortable Ottenberg!" I hear him say, his Texan accent further accentuating the mocking drawl in his words. He kneels down so that his bloated, red, Texan face is right next to mine. His expression shifts to something hard and horrible. "The way I see it, you're as good as off this boat!"

CHAPTER VIII

"Ouch!" I whine as Ally realigns my broken nose with a sharp tug and pushes a ball of cotton up each of my nostrils to stop the bleeding.

"Don't be such a bleedin' baby!" I take a second out of my schedule of being miserable and look at her reproachfully without putting my head back down. The fact that I don't even mock her for this poor pun speaks volumes about my situation.

I am sitting on a gurney in the Dolos' med-bay, my bedsheet, which I have found again once I re-learned which way was up, dutifully tugged around my waist. Haru isn't here. Since she wasn't busy collecting her dignity back up from the ground, Marlon dragged her to see the Captain once she got dressed and told me to stay put in the medbay.

Ally had taken care of my broken nose while simultaneously scolding me for bleeding all over her precious med bay. "Keep your head back until the bleeding stops," she finally tells me and pulls off the rubber gloves before she throws them into the bin alongside the dressing material she used. "So, you and Haru huh?" She grins at me.

"Jesus, word travels fast!" "I don't know about word, but it was kinda hard NOT to hear Steve shouting about it." I try to blow air through my nose in sarcastic agreement but a sharp pain reminds me that my nose is broken and plugged with cotton right now. I feel sorry for myself for a second. "Well it is not like I didn't suspect it." she grins. "You, always eyeballing her and such. To be honest, I was just waiting for you guys to invite me for a bit of a threeway party." I chuckle. "The way you fuck around Ally, there is no telling if you're clean!" "Fuck you Kev! You know you want to tap that ass!" She mockingly slaps he butt and we both have a laugh at that. A laugh that dies off way too quickly. "I feel bad for her," I finally say, my voice nasally distorted by the cotton. "Marlon's gonna shit all over her just to get to me!" Ally crosses her arms in front of her chest and looks at me sternly. "You know, Steve is not as big of an asshole as you always try to make him out to be!" I jab a finger pointedly at my broken nose and smuggly arch my eyebrows. "Yeah, he doesn't like you obviously, but be fair, how often do you give him crap?" She lets her gaze fall to the floor and hugs herself tighter. "And we're all on edge with this messed up tourist business."

Oh hello there, elephant in the room, did you just fart? With Haru's visit to my cabin and then the whole broken nose business, I had almost forgotten about the shitty situation we were in. Ally and I stand in silence for a moment. Her looking at the floor, me intently watching the ceiling. "Say Ally, can you give me some painkillers or something? This broken nose thing gets old fast!" She jerks her head up and looks at me with wide eyes for a second. "Not really" she admits sheepishly. "Look," she starts to explain defensively as a response to my unvoiced "Why the fuck not?" stare. "You know how I told Steve I couldn't prepare Preemie cocktails for them all because of short supplies?" I nod and immediately regret it as my nose apparently also hurts when moving my neck. "Let's just say, the Captain isn't the only one on board the Dolos who runs an "optimised" profit center." Ally shoots me an unconvincing smile.

"What are you saying Ally?" "I might have sold all of our medical supplies at Dionysus Port to make a few extra bucks." She looks at me with pleading eyes. "Please don't tell anyone!" "Ally, what about my situation looks like I can afford to keep any more secrets from the Captain." I jump off the gurney and look directly at her. "Are you insane?" "Hey it is not like we need those meds in the first place. We're asleep most of the trip anyways." She starts pacing in front of me and suddenly looks a lot younger than normal. "And I got stupid and had to pay off a wee gambling bet." "How much are we talking about Ally?" She swallows hard and stops pacing. "Fifty grand" "Fucking hell, Ally!" My hand travels up to rub the back of my nose in annoyance, but I catch myself halfway. Probably not a good idea right now. "Ally, we found the tourist in a container with medical supplies." I tell her and watch her slowly realize what that means. "Shit! You think…" "I don't know what to think Ally, but we need to tell the Captain!" The words taste sour in my mouth. "YOU, need to tell the Captain!" Ally sinks to the floor and leans against the wall, running her hand through her hair over and over again. "This was not what I wanted. Nobody was supposed to get hurt!" she's talking more to herself than to me now. "I would have quietly restocked in the next port and nobody would have been the wiser." I slowly lower myself next to her, careful not to further agitate my nose or lose the bedsheet around my waist. I put my arm around her. "Nobody could have foreseen this Ally." We both stare blankly in front of us, looking at nothing in particular.

CHAPTER IX

Not long after, the Captain enters the med bay. Okay, time to face the music. Ally and I get up. "Ally, would you mind letting Kevin and me have a word in private for a minute?" It is voiced as a question, but Ally and I both know that it is anything but. Ally nods and leaves. Before she closes the door her eyes find mine and she smiles sheepishly at me. God, do I not want to be me right now. "So," the Captain starts and stops at the same time. I get the feeling she is not really sure how to start this conversation either. That's not like her... odd.

"So" I pick up where she left off, "I take it you and XO Marlon had a chat." "About physical violence between shipmates, yes." She shoots me an apologetic smile. "I docked his pay for this trip and he will have to apologize to you. I can't have people knocking each other out. What kind of working environment is that?" "That implies it would still be a working environment for me going forward?" I am confused. She nods and looks at me sternly. "I'm going to be frank with you Kevin. It is hard to get good people. And as much as I don't want to admit it, both you and Haruto are more than capable in your respective jobs. I simply cannot afford to lose even one of you."

"Thank y–" The Captain puts a hand up telling me to shut it. "That doesn't mean that I am not pissed off about the fact that you ignored one of my two rules. I seriously resent you for putting me in this situation!" I see where this is going. "I am not going to break it off with her!" "Then I am going to dock both of your pays by forty percent until you do!" She crosses her arms in front of her chest, her tone final. "If that is what it takes. So be it!"

I've known the Captain long enough to know when there is no arguing with her. You need to pick your battles and this is not a hill I am choosing to die on. She starts to grin. "Well shit Kevin, of all the girls in the galaxy!" I look at her confused.

"I had the same conversation with Haruto." Her grin changes into a genuine smile. "And the same exact outcome." She puts her hand on my shoulder and nods to me reassuringly. "I don't like my crew to hook up because I don't want people to fuck all over the ship like bunnies. This is a workplace and not a space faring swinger club. As a Captain I have to object to your relationship. As a friend… damn Kevin it is about fucking time!" I smile back at her. "Thanks Captain. So… you're not gonna dock our pay?" She laughs out loudly. "Oh I am so gonna dock your pay. Nobody will respect the rules if there are no consequences breaking them!" She chuckles and shakes her head. "But you get to experience that cut in pay knowing that you have my blessing." She makes a show of crossing herself. I shake my head and flinch as the motion agitates my broken nose. A pang of sympathy mixed with a bit of guilt flashes across the Captain's face. "I am genuinely sorry about that." she gestures towards my nose. "Didn't Ally give you something for the pain?" "Nah, it is fine." There, dodged the question. Chickened out of it like a pro. Let Ally handle Ally-business.

"Oookay." She looks confused. "Well, with all this mushy

shit out of the way…" The Captain puts her left hand in her pocket and produces a small chip with what seems like a wireless interface attached to it and puts it in front of me on the gurney.

"Before you and Steve had your little boxing match, he actually wanted to talk to you about this." I pick up the piece and turn it around between my fingers. The whole thing is maybe the size of a fingernail.

"What's that?" "I was hoping you can tell me!" I give it a closer look. "Well it is a data chip with a wireless interface, but you don't need me to tell you that." She crosses her arms in front of her chest again. Her eyes trained on my face. "Is there any place on the Dolos where we use such a thing?"I shake my head. My nose hurts. I ignore it.

"Do we use parts of it?" "You want to know if someone could have constructed this by salvaging other pieces?" She nods. "The wireless interface, yes. That is the standard piece for pretty much every component we use on the Dolos that is either sending or receiving data. But the chip is a completely different brand from what we normally use. In fact, I make it a point to avoid this particular brand, as they are prone to failure in the long run." The Captain audibly releases a breath and her whole body language relaxes. "So it had to come from an external source." "I'd say so yeah." She puts both of her hands on my shoulders and looks directly into my eyes. "I need you to be a hundred percent sure about this Kevin!" I take a thorough look at the chip again and take my time with it. After a rough minute, I nod.

"Yes Captain, I am a hundred percent sure. Where did you get it from?" The Captain takes the device from my hand and puts it back in her pocket.

"Steve found it magnetized to the inside of the tourist cryo chamber. He thinks it transmitted the faulty code that piggybacked on the Preemie routine." I cock my head sideways. "Hold on. He mentioned an unregulated update of the cryo software before." "Exactly. That little fucker," the Captain points at her pocket, "forced the system to accept the new code disguised as a system update." I could see that the Captain was visibly elated at this new development. That little device made it a lot less likely that one of the crew was involved in this whole mess. A bitter part of me thinks she is desperately grasping at straws. Who can blame her though.

CHAPTER X

About two hours later, the searing pain in my nose has turned to a dull but persistent throb and for the third time in twenty-four hours I find myself part of an all-hands meeting in the common area of the Dolos. I only listen half-heartedly as the Captain updates everyone on the hack caused by the device found in the tourist's cryo pod.

"That by itself would be almost enough evidence, but there is more that supports the theory of our tourist looking to score medical supplies and steer the Dolos towards his pirate buddies."

Ally shifts uncomfortably at the mention of the medical supplies. Taking a closer look at her, I can see that she cried. A lot. I get a queasy feeling in my gut. It takes a lot to make Ally cry. A lot more to make her not care who notices her doing so. "As we've found the body of our tourist in a container with medical supplies, the only valid theory I can come up with is that there is a third party involved somewhere in the cargo hold that, for whatever reason, was opposed to the interference with that specific container." The Captain takes her time to look reassuringly from one crew member to the other. "Thankfully, that means that none of the crew was directly involved in this business and quite frankly, I am keen on putting this mess behind us. Every hour we are out of cryo takes a cut out of our profits, so that being said, I shall invoke the right of martial law any Captain has on their ship. We're going to open the cargo bay doors and suck the atmosphere out of it, spacing whoever is hiding in it alongside their agenda and go back into cryo to end this mess!" Everyone mumbles more or less coherent words of agreement. "Steve, how much longer till you get the cryo system working flawlessly again?" The Captain looks at the XO, who makes it a point to look at anything and anyone but me. "Couple of hours at most. Now that I know where the interference came from, I can easily remove it. Worst case scenario, I backup the system before the "update" and we're fine!" The Captain nods and takes a deep breath. Her face sombers up. "Now with the business end taken care of, as most of you should be aware by now, there were a couple of transgressions among the crew that we need to address." She looks at me and then at XO Marlon. "There was a physical altercation between Steve and Kevin. Apart from a significant fee, Steve will apologize to Kevin, and I expect both of you to clear your differences going forward!" Marlon looks at me with the same expression you look at a half-rotten corpse and mumbles "I am sorry" under his breath. I try not to look at him and nod sharply as a form of acknowledgement. "Jesus Christ, I expect you to repeat that after this meeting in a more sincere manner Steve!" the Captain snaps at the XO, like he is a little boy who was caught with his hand in the cookie jar.

Marlon tries to shoot her a murderous look but can't bring himself to commit to it. "Further, it has come to my attention that Kevin and Haruto have been in a relationship, despite my explicit rule against such a thing on this ship. As long as their relationship is ongoing, they will receive a significant dock to their pay going forward.

They both agreed to this separately as an alternative to ending their employment on the Dolos."

The Captain looks first at me and then at Haru with a warm smile. She takes another deep breath and her smile falters quickly. "Which brings me to the last altercation that has happened, which unfortunately requires more drastic measures."

Out of the corner of my eye, I see Ally tense up. I look at her and then at the Captain. My eyes widen. "It is highly likely that our current situation was – at least partly – caused by Ally not only interacting with certain criminal elements, but also encouraging them to further mess with us by selling off our medical supplies at Dionysus Port. In doing so, she has not only cost us precious money and time clearing up this mess outside of cryo, but also put the entire ship and crew in danger. I appreciate Ally coming forward with this by herself, which is the only reason I will not report her to the officials once we dock. However I cannot in good conscience keep Ally in my employment."

I voice a toneless "No" and shake my head. I know what is coming next but I still don't want to hear it.

"Don't think that this was an easy decision, but I decided to terminate Ally's employment contract. You are expected to leave the Dolos as soon as we dock at the next port and are to be confined to either your cryo pod or your cabin until you do so." The Captain pauses to let this sink in. The silence is almost smothering all of us. A silent sob from Ally and the dull background hum of the Dolos' engine are the only sounds for a long time. I am struggling to grasp the concept of what was just said. Haru gets up and hugs Ally, both women crying. Marlon is looking pointedly to the floor, his eyes a million miles away. I find I don't know what to do with my hands as my body is desperate to move somewhere while my mind does not know where to. I end up fidgeting weirdly in place. "I am really sorry Ally, but I don't see any other way," the Captain croaks as her voice betrays her. She hurriedly walks out of the common area. I catch a glimpse of tears as I watch her leave.

A second later Marlon snaps into movement and leaves the common area as well. Probably to get the cryo system up and running again.

CHAPTER XI

The next couple of hours pass in a blur. Haru and I escort Ally to her cabin and can't bring ourselves to leave her alone. We both have been friends with Ally subjectively for several years, objectively for a couple of centuries at least. The fact that we won't see her again after she steps off the Dolos doesn't feel real to us yet. At one point, the Captain hails me to help her override the cargo hold doors, so that we can open them without being docked, venting all the air out of the cargo hold. We leave them open for several hours to make sure that anything living outside of sealed containers dies in the vacuum.

To her credit, the Captain does not try to strike up a conversation with me while we work. I am not entirely sure if I would have obliged her. At this point, I cannot tell who I resent more, her or myself. The Captain dismisses me and I walk back to Ally's cabin. If I hadn't brought the topic up with Ally, she would have never, ever told the Captain about her mishap. On the other side, we wouldn't have been able to put this situation behind us. Did we put it behind us? It doesn't feel like it. Our little family is torn wide open. The immediate situation might be resolved, but at the end of the day, at the end of this trip, Ally is still going to leave, and while we are on our way to our next destination, all tucked in and wrapped up tight in our cryo pods, Ally will age and die, either in a world she does not and cannot understand anymore, or on board of another freighter, away from the rest of us. What do you say to someone in that situation? How can you possibly do right by that person without sounding like a massive hypocrite? For once, there is no banter between us. Ally is sitting on the floor of her cabin, Haru on one side, me on the other, all of us staring at the floor, our eyes far away.

At the beginning there was a lot of crying, but like with any real tragedy, at some point the tears stopped, replaced by that horrible feeling of utter helplessness. That tight feeling in your stomach as if someone punched you hard, right in the belly. A part of my brain screams at me that we should be making the most of these last couple of hours together, but that part is quickly drowned out by self-loathing, guilt and fear. At some point the Captain hails again. This time she summons Haru. I barely recognize the voice over the intercom in my stupor. It is only when Haru starts to get up that my trancelike isolation bubble bursts. "Are you going to be okay?" she asks Ally. Her eyes wander from Ally to me, addressing the question to me as well. My eyes widen and I allow myself the hint of a nod. Ally just sobs – the dry-heave sob of someone who's body is utterly exhausted from crying. Haru kneels down and hugs us both before she gets up she turns her head. "I'll be back in a sec!" she whispers in my ear, and I cherish the feeling of her close to me. She opens the cabin door. Looking back, she voices a silent "I love you" before she closes the door again, and all of a sudden it is just Ally and me. "I am sorry Ally!" No response, not even a shift in her body language.

"I am so fucking sorry!" I am not entirely sure if I am talking to her or to myself. Ally noisily sniffles her nose. "Not your fault," is all she manages to say, her voice heavy with strain. "I didn't think the Captain would go this far…"

Ally lets out a bitter chuckle. "Shit Kev, thinking has never been your strong suit!" We both have a laugh at that, grasping at the thin straw of normality that odd remark represents. Desperately trying to cling to it as it fades out again. We both fall quiet way too quickly. "Quite frankly, I think I am the one person on this boat who can manage to stay in port for a while." Ally smiles sadly. "I will miss you guys though." Her voice tightens and she starts to cry again. Heavy sobs shake her. I put my arm around her and she clings to me like her life depends on it. At long last something inside me gives way and I finally start to cry as well.

We sit there, on the floor of her cabin, bawling our eyes out. I don't know how much time passes, but Haruto doesn't come back. Ally alternates between crying and sitting in silence. Nothing exists but this very cabin. If there has ever been a world around it, I wouldn't know any longer. I feel sorry for Ally. But in an egoistical, horrible part of my soul, I know I feel even more sorry for myself. I might not want to admit it but this is my fault. I fucked it up. All I wanted to do is keep this ship, this crew, this family afloat! And with every action I took, I made even more sure that we ended up split and hurting. Ally got the worst of all. It should have been me, not her! "Kevin, please escort Ally to the common room!" I shake my head as I need a moment to realize that the Captain was speaking to me from the speaker. "Kevin? Do you hear me?" I jump up and look at Ally, who in turn is looking at me, confused. There is an odd glimmer in her eyes. Hoping against hope that this new development might deter her fate. "On our way Captain!" I croak and move on to help Ally up. As I enter the common room, I see the rest of the crew are already assembled. The Captain and Marlon are standing in the middle of the room, uneasy and tense. Haru is sitting at the table, her eyes unfocused and far away. When I enter, she looks at me and quickly looks away. When I try to look at her again, her eyes keep avoiding my gaze.

The whole room feels off somehow. "What's this about Captain?" I look from one of the crew to the next. Marlon moves and helps Ally sit down. Am I imagining things or is he trying to stand between me and the doorway? The Captain takes a long, hard look at me. Her eyes full of intense, cold determination. When she finally speaks, her voice lacks any of the humor and maternal flair it normally carries.

"Why did you kill the tourist Kevin?"

CHAPTER XII

"What?" My heart is beating a million times a minute, my mind going through emotions equally fast – confusion, fear, humour, relief, terror... "I know you did it." The Captain, again with that hardened voice. "I just don't know why." I let out a fake laugh, trying to make light of the situation, and fail. "Captain, is this some kind of joke?" Nobody is laughing. I look from crew member to crew member. The Captain keeps staring daggers at me. Haru avoids my gaze, Ally is confused and Marlon... if looks could kill, I would have been dead and buried five minutes ago. "Is this about the thirty-six hours I was asleep during my Preemie cycle?" "It started with that!" This time it is Marlon talking, his Texan drawl turned down to a menacing whisper as he approaches me. I try to back away but he quickly has me with my back to the wall. "Ally is a lot of things, but she isn't stupid." he says, never taking his eyes off of me. "She would never go as far as to endanger the crew. So, when this whole tourist mess cleared up so perfectly, I had my doubts." "Doubts? Hell Marlon, looks more like conjecture to me!" I snap at him, my mind settling on aggression as a measure of defence. "You've

been trying to pin this fucking thing on me ever since the start!" Marlon lets out a cruel chuckle. "Well Ottenberg, I don't need to try anymore!" Marlon looks at the Captain and she nods, her eyes never leaving mine. "The whole situation was a bit too clean for my taste, so when Maria… when the Captain ordered me to get the cryo system running again, I took a last look at the cryo protocols, and with a little bit of extra motivation, I was finally able to unscramble the timeline." He pulls out the small device from his pocket. "You see, it is a lot easier to counteract hacks if you have the source code." Marlon throws the device at my feet. "Imagine my surprise when I saw the time difference between the decanting of your cryo pod, the tourist's pod, and the Captain's pod." I wait for him to continue, but he doesn't. Looking at the Captain again, I try to voice my frustration, but she cuts me off. "You told us that you decanted, slept for up to thirty-six hours, realized the tourist was awake, and then you decanted me." She paused and closed her eyes, a flicker of sadness running over her face. "Even if we apply a margin for error, we're looking at a maximum of seventy-two hours." "According to the cryo protocol however, you waited a full six days to decant the Captain." Marlon steps closer to me again, ignoring any common rule of personal space. His bloated, red face directly next to mine, I can feel his hot breath on my cheek. "That is it?" I ask, trying my hardest to keep my voice from cracking as I unsuccessfully try to back away from Marlon even further. "You accuse me of killing the tourist based on THAT? Are we sure that you even completely restored the protocol? Or that you are not trying to implicate me on purpose?" I almost scream the last part. "We couldn't be sure no," the Captain chimes back in, her voice losing some of the steel in it. "Which is why I rechecked all other components."
This is not good. Not good at all. "Turns out the container we found the tourist in was accessed long after your assumed thirty-six hours sleep break. And long before

someone altered our course and set off the transmission." The Captain takes another deep breath. "Turns out both the course alteration and the transmission were executed shortly before my decanting, using your user profile." We stare at each other. The Captain looks at me with a sad expression. "The device scrambled the whole cryo system? Who says it didn't scramble other systems as well?" My voice breaks almost hysterically. "It could have been manufactured to resemble my user profile!" "It wasn't" A quiet voice cuts through the tension. We all look in the direction of the speaker. It was Haru. I close my eyes as my stomach takes a tumble. "I checked it myself. Several times. Because I couldn't believe it." she continues in the same voiceless, sad tone. "But it was you Kevin."

With these words, she turns her gaze towards me. These eyes I found myself looking into so often during our secret post-cryo dates, streaked with tears, full of emotion. Hurt, betrayal, denial, anger. For a moment, everything else vanishes. It is just me and Haru in a black void. Her eyes asking the question her mind dares not to pose. Did I do it? Did I kill the tourist? I am afraid it is true. All fight and defiance vanishes from my body as I slump down the wall wanting to curl up into a ball. Before averting my gaze, I can see the beginning of something terrible form in Haru's eyes. She sits up and storms across the room, slapping me sharp across the face. I can't bring myself to look at her. Shame burns hotter on my face than the mark her hand leaves on my cheek. She stands in front of me for an awkward moment, probably debating if she is done hitting me. I feel a part of me tear as she finally turns around and storms out of the common room. "I guess that is as much of a confession as we're gonna get from him," I hear the XO say from somewhere far away. Marlon slaps a cable binder around my wrists, locking them into place behind my back. I hear them agreeing on dumping me in my cabin for now before interrogating me further, but my mind does not compute the fact until I hit the floor of my cabin, hard. Without so much as a word, Marlon locks the door behind me.

CHAPTER XIII

Have you ever asked yourself if you could kill someone? Truly and purposefully end another person's life? Have you asked yourself what it would take for you to do so? What price would it cost? What part of you are you willing to give in order to take? I never did. Quite frankly, I was happy with my small, unimportant life. I had a good thing going with Haru. A small but constant number of relationships that I cherished. I was never an ambitious man. I never fell into the trap a lot of people do – the quest for happiness. I was happy being content, being of use. My life wasn't perfect, but it didn't have to be. Most of the time, I knew what went where and what role to play in the bigger scheme of things. I was a roleplayer and perfectly aware of that. But I was comfortable in my role. Not all of us get to be "special". We don't need to be. The Dolos, this ugly, old freighter with this rugged handful of souls on it was my home, my family. I had a place here. A place where I felt wanted, needed, liked. A place I understood. A place that understood me. Wouldn't you fight for such a place? They come for me about an hour later. I hear their footsteps on the corridor outside the cabin long before the old rusty lock turns and the door swings open. "Rise and shine, sunshine!" Marlon snarls and picks me up as roughly as possible. He tosses me onto my cot and I try to assume some form of sitting position. "Just the two of you?" I croak, looking at the Captain and Marlon. "I don't think Haruto wants to see you pal," Marlon's face is all business. A part of me would feel better if he'd be his usual, insufferable self.

"Ally is still confined to her cabin," the Captain adds, her voice carefully neutral. Looking at her, she has aged a couple of years over the last hour. "Well if there is any upside from this, I can at least right that one." I say trying to prepare myself for what is to come. "She had nothing to do with the whole thing on board. Her only crime is selling off the medical supplies." The Captain arches an eyebrow at me. "If there is any truth in that I will revisit her situation." She looks at Marlon. "For now, I need to know what happened after you decanted, Kevin. And this time the truth!" I try to sit as comfortably as possible with my arms tied behind my back and straighten my back. "I didn't lie to you outright," I start and catch a "Bullshit!" and a hard flat right hand to the face from Marlon. Picking myself up again I can see a quick flash of anger in the Captain's face, aimed at Marlon. "Go on" she utters from behind clenched teeth. "I woke up as the Preemie, took Ally's cocktail and legitimately was out for thirty-six hours. I did not notice the tourist decanting, or that anything was off."

I felt around the inside of my mouth with my tongue, having the suspicion that Marlon's last slap had cut open something as my mouth filled with the taste of copper. "I was going to decant the rest of the crew and then speed up Haru's decanting so that we could have a couple of days for ourselves before the rest of you guys came up to speed." "He did that everytime he was Preemie Maria; I showed you the protocols of the last couple of trips," Marlon injected himself. The Captain nodded and urged me to keep going. "It wasn't until the cryo system told me that it was way too early in the trip to wake up the rest of the crew that I realized the tourist's pod was open…"

CHAPTER XIV

I stare dumbfounded at the empty cryo pod, painfully aware of the last dull throb of the Preemie hangover headache slowing down my thought process. It takes me the better part of a minute to compute what I am seeing. I stumble over to the empty pod. Nothing seems off or out of place. No sign of a malfunction. No sign of force. It is simply open and empty. It should not be open and empty. "What the hell is going on?" I mumble to myself as I look around the cryo bay, feeling a bit lost. Lost in Space. Hah! That would be hilarious if I weren't so confused right now. I shuffle back to the cryo controls and try to coax the AI into telling me the decanting date of the tourist's pod. The entry is really scrambled by the wireless device's introduced forced re-write. At this point in time I don't know that yet though, so I try to work around the scrambled system. "Status report of cryo_pod_backup?" Cryo_pod_backup status = inactive "Yeah no shit buddy." I massage the back of my nose and try to think. I access the pod's status a day after we launched. Cryo_pod_backup status = active Alright, so it isn't a sensor malfunction. "Status report of cryo_pod_backup at time of last execute of decant_crew_preemie.exe?" Cryo_pod_backup status = active So our tourist was still in cryo when I woke up. Son of a bitch. Ally's cocktail knocked me out something fierce. "Time since last change of "status" for cryo_pod_backup?" [1] D - [14] H - [48] M I check the AI protocol for the timespan of my decanting. The tourist was decanted an hour after me. I must have barely fallen asleep when he woke up. I leave the cryo chamber, go to the Dolos' bridge and cross reference both the current position in our flight path as well as the timeframe with the main system. To my dismay, there is no discrepancy. Slowly it is starting to hit me. I am not alone on the Dolos. I can feel the wretched feeling of terror bubble in the back of my mind. If it had been a simple malfunction, I would have encountered an equally cryo hungover tourist somewhere in the ship by now. But I didn't, so whoever woke up an hour after me was either drugged up or conditioned to shake off the effects of an unassisted decanting long enough to get past me and out of sight. I jerk upright and slam the door to the bridge shut, locking myself in. I am shaking at the thought that I was just lying there, out cold, while whoever the fuck our tourist is, walked past me. He could have gotten rid of me then and there, and I wouldn't even have noticed it. "Alright Kevin, you can't keep sitting on the bridge like some asshole, you need to figure this shit out." I open the bridge interface console again and let the main system list all accessed programs, scripts and routines since it came back online. Two-thousand three-hundred and forty-eight entries. I go through them carefully, line by line. Most of the entries are the normal start-up routines I triggered by booting up the main system after decanting: Life support, sensors, navigations, engines, the works, followed by various diagnostic routines, the ship taking a good long look at itself in the mirror, checking for failures or damage. After that, it goes into the simple actions I have undertaken, from various door accesses to brewing coffee to accessing the cryostasis system. Everything is there. One entry peaks my interest. I did not access the cargo bay hub panel, yet there it is. Not even twelve hours after my decanting, someone had messed with the panel in the cargo bay. I go back over the various door access entries and can construct a way from the cryo chamber to the cargo hold. Whoever made their way to the cargo bay, it wasn't me. "Gotcha, motherfucker!" I lick my lips and check the list again. Nobody had triggered the door to the cargo hold after the interaction with the panel, meaning our little sleepwalker of a tourist hasn't left. I remotely lock the door to the hold and get to work. A couple of minutes later, I enter the cargo bay, wrapped in several layers of t-shirts and pullovers and armed with a big kitchen knife from the common room. The knife is more for moral support. Whoever is in here can hear me coming from literally a mile away. If they want to get the drop on me, they can do so easily. I make my way undisturbed towards the central cargo hub panel and check what was accessed. I find what I am looking for and follow the guidance lights until I am in front of a container. Not the medical supplies container we would investigate a couple of days later, but the extravagant, grey container next to it. The one that looks like it was really new and really expensive. There is no question our tourist has accessed it. He has done something to it, so that a keypad was accessible and the door is no longer closed, only closed over. With trembling hands (only partly due to the cold I have to admit grudgingly), I slowly open the door. Fluorescent light spills out from the container. I clear the door enough to get through and step – knife raised – into the container. The inside looks like a high-tech laboratory, all shiny aluminium and white plastic surfaces. In the middle of the container, held in place by two massive cargo girders, is some sort of shuttle. I have never seen a design like this. It is obviously a more contemporary design. Nothing even close to this shuttle has ever docked at a spaceport I was visiting. Next to it, in between one of the cargo girders and an access console, I find our tourist. Sitting with his back to the shuttle, his knees pulled up to his chest and – my heart starts racing as soon as I see it – cradling a gun. I suck in air through my teeth and try to back away. The second I flinch away from him, the tourist comes alive. It takes him a split second to recognize the situation, and before I know it he jumps to his feet and points the gun's business end at me. I raise my hands and drop the knife. "Good morning sunshine!" I try to quip, but the humor sticks to the back of my throat. The statement sounds more like a question and less like the dry wit remark I was going for. The tourist blinks a couple of times as his eyes glaze over for a second. He is still feeling the cryo hangover himself. He steps towards me and uses his foot to kick the knife away from me. His movements feel sluggish from cryo sickness, but there is a certain focussed quality to them. Every little move he makes seems like a deliberate, precise motion. I don't like it at all. "Dwight was it, right?" "Shut up!" Well I guess we're not going to have a conversation. I swallow hard. The tourist – Dwight – checks the access panel. He tries his best to put his body between me and the screen, but I can see some sort of progress bar.

"What are you downloading?" My mouth is quicker than my brain, and I curse myself as Dwight focusses back on me and trains the gun at my head. "How are you up so quickly?" His voice is calm and measured. It terrifies me even more. "What do you mean?" "You are this trip's Preemie, you should be out for at least another twelve hours." I shoot him a confused look "Quite frankly dude, YOU shouldn't be awake at all." Dwight steps towards me and puts the gun's muzzle against my forehead. "I don't like to repeat myself!" he snarls and gives me a look that makes me almost pee my pants. "I had a cocktail from our doc to help me get over the hangover myself. Please, I am not a curious person, I just wanted to know where you went off to… ohmagawdIdontwanttodie…" I'd like to tell you that I'm weathering this situation like a calm, collected, professional human being, but the truth of it is, I never had a gun to my head before. Hell I've never ever SEEN a gun in real life before. I'm losing it, big time. Within minutes, I am reduced to a terrified, sobbing mess. Dwight obviously deduces from my astonishing poker face that I am no threat to him and puts the gun in his belt. His attention focussed back on the access panel. The progress bar fills fully, and once it has done so, Dwight pulls another wireless gadget off the panel and turns back to me. "What is your name?" "Kevin." I try my damnedest to keep my voice from cracking. "Okay Kevin, there are two possible ways this can go." He looks me straight in the eye and his voice takes on a steely quality. "I don't want to hurt you, but if you mess this job up for me, I will put a bullet in your brain and put you in an airlock. Do you want to be put in an airlock Kevin?" I shake my head dumbfounded. "I figured as much. The alternative is you forget this situation, we both get back into cryo and finish this trip. You never saw me up, you never saw me in this container, you never saw all of this!" Dwight waves an arm around the interior of the container. "We all die of old age a long time from now!" I swallow hard. "That sounds like a kickass plan." I slowly find my wits again as terror is replaced with a sense of fatal urgency. "Shame I emergency locked the cryo bay before I came to find you." Dwight cocks his head and looks at me, narrowing his eyes.

"That has logged all interaction with containers and panels, and there is no way I can erase those." Dwight takes a deep breath. "That makes things… interesting." To my surprise, he lowers the gun and sits back down, his back to the shuttle. He rubs his temples, and some of the tension eases out of his shoulders.

"Relax Kevin, I am not going to shoot you." He realizes I am looking at him confused and chuckles. "Sit down man,

I was talking a big game to scare you off, but that's not much use now is it?" I sit down across from him. "So, no matter what we do, whoever checks the logs will see what happened and what we accessed?" I nod. A quick frown crosses his face. "What were you accessing anyways?" I ask, amazed at how quickly I regained my wits. Dwight nods towards the shuttle. "This baby right here is a new prototype. I was supposed to get out of cryo early, get the plans, go back into cryo without anyone noticing, drop the plans off at the next spaceport, get paid. Easy money." "How'd you plan on going back into cryo undetected?" "Quite frankly, I thought you would be out a couple of hours longer, maybe a day. By the time you'd shrug off your cryo sickness I'd be back in the tube." Dwight takes a deep breath and flashes a lazy grin. "I figured eventually, you'd just note down the whole early release from cryo as a malfunction and go back to sleep. How was I supposed to know I wasn't the only one with anti-hangover drugs." I let out a whistle. "Been wondering how you were up and functioning this quickly." "Had a friend of mine at Dionysus Port stash a bit of a cocktail for me." Dwight points at the gun in his belt. "Alongside this beauty. Was a bitch to get to though. Had to get all the way to the cargo bay before I could get my fix!" We sit in silence for a couple of minutes. "So I take it you're getting paid royally if you're taking a thirty year trip?" Dwight nods, his eyes on me. I think we both know where this is going to go. Eventually, we will make a deal and I might find myself the recipient of a sizable bonus, on top of what the Captain is paying me. "What kind of prototype is this shuttle that someone is willing to pay out of the ass for blueprints anyways?" He looks at the shuttle behind him. "Apparently, it has a new type of engine that gets you from one end of the galaxy to the other within hours." "Bullshit!" The engineer in me takes over. Dwight shrugs. "Hey man, I am not the brains behind this operation, I just get the plans. Someone else does the heavy lifting." I try to recall all kinds of physical theories that have been released over the years. "Mind if I take a look at the plans?" I have to admit, I am curious. Even an engineer without ambition is an engineer when it comes down to it. Dwight nods and points towards the access panel.I step up and start going through the plans.

CHAPTER XV

"This might actually work." I rub the back of my nose and step away from the panel roughly an hour later. My head is spinning at what I'd just looked at. I don't pretend to understand all of it, I am just a lowly LSCT engineer after all, but I am an engineer. And from what I understood, this prototype, this Particle-Zero drive, could boil down a thirty year cryo trip to roughly half a week, maybe less. It wouldn't even require the crew to be in cryo. How the hell was this possible? "This prototype isn't the first iteration. Whoever built this has sunk some serious time and resources into this technology," I mumble more to myself than to Dwight. "Why the fuck does nobody know this drive exists?" Dwight lets out a humourless snicker. "Why? Think for a second Kevin. Over the centuries, the Lost have become a self-contained workforce. They don't vote, they don't take up a lot of resources and they recycle any money they get paid by spending them in the spaceports." Dwight pauses to see if I am still with him. "Sure it takes a long time for you guys to get from A to B, but that just benefits the people in charge more, as they have enough time to build around the supply and demand and make sure they end up wealthy and in charge. Why would they want to change that?" I barely listen to him. "This technology changes everything," I state the obvious. Dwight stops explaining, realizing I am having my own conversation in my head. He looks at me concerned. "Dude, are you okay?" I am not. I am one of the Lost. I am one of the crew of the Dolos. I don't know anything about nor do I care for what society is like. I am happy in my microbubble, where my biggest concern and fear is if XO Dickhead likes me or not. This ship, this crew, this system is my safespace. How the hell am I supposed to function if all of this ends? I have no family anymore. Never had much to begin with. I am not social. The bare amount of social interaction between crew members is almost too much for me. And what of the rest of the crew. Ally would thrive, she would find a way to be out and about while still being on her own in no time. And Haru? She is someone who adapts really quickly. She'd be gone and moving on from her loser Lost ex-boyfriend. And what then? I'd be alone. Really alone. In a society I don't understand. My whole skillset rendered useless. Ironically, truly lost. "Hey man, I asked if you are okay?" Dwight repeats and shakes me. I slowly get back to reality and look at him, not quite believing that all of this is happening. "You're not gonna go all crazy on me now will you?" "The guy you work for…" I mumble, more to myself than to him. "He's going to make these plans public?" Dwight looks at me with an exception you give a kid that just declared "the grass is green" with utter surprise. "Duh!" He nods. "Everything will change then." "Obviously, but for the better. No more thirty year cryo naps man, don't tell me that doesn't sound appealing to you." I think of the crew sitting together in the common room, joking and laughing together. I think of Ally and me flirtatiously bantering back and forth. I think of long Preemie shifts sitting in front of a display running some discontinued soap opera, huddling in my thermo blankets and genuinely being happy. I think of the sensation of Haru's hand in mine, the sensation of her head leaning on my shoulder during our secret cryo dates. I look on in surprise as I somehow manage to have Dwight's gun in my hand. A mental image of Haru smiling at me over her shoulder. A sense of home. A sense of belonging.

"I am sorry." I pull the trigger. Nobody can ever know about this...

CHAPTER XVI

It is silent in my bunk for a long time. Both the Captain and Marlon look intensely at the floor not trying how to react to my confession. "What then?" the Captain eventually speaks up, her voice coarse. "I panicked. Quite a lot. But eventually, I tried to cover everything up. Dragged the body out of the container, sealed it again, hard re-booted the ship's main system to get access to the logs and forged the whole medical supply narrative." I can't bring myself to meet her eyes. "So you willingly incriminated Ally?" There is a tense quality of anger to the Captain's voice now. "No." My voice is barely more than a whisper now. "I had no idea what she was up to, otherwise I hadn't fabricated that whole business with the medical supply container. I looked at the shipping manifest and chose the first thing I found that would even remotely justify some sort of illegal activity." Another couple of moments pass as none of us can say something. "I never wanted to hurt anyone." "You killed someone Kevin!" The Captain's bluntness hurts more than Marlons' slaps. "He would have changed everything!" I honestly don't know if I say this out loud or just think it. "There would be no need for the Lost anymore Captain. It would have torn the crew apart!" She looks at me, her eyes hard and cold. "And what exactly have you done?" Her statement, her tone, her voice, one diamond cut to the core of my existence. I feel like the room is spinning. "I should throw you out of the airlock for everything you did Kevin. And the goddamn container right alongside your sorry ass!" When she looks at me, there is only harsh, cold hatred. "Put him in cryo. We hand him over to the authorities at the next spaceport," she utters to Marlon and leaves the room, not sparing me another glance or word. I feel like the floor is moving as I lose equilibrium and slam on the floor, face first. I register that my already broken nose is sending searing agony towards my brain, but I no longer care. I realize that Marlon is lifting me up, surprisingly gentle, as if it would happen to another person. I am put in my cryo pod. Everything's on auto pilot. I see a quick glance of Ally who administers the cryo drugs. If there is one upside to this whole mess, it's that she gets to stay on the ship now. She hesitates, and for a second it looks like she will give me a hug, but she decides against it and leaves. I never get to see Haru again. For the first time in centuries, I welcome the dreamless state of cryostasis. Coming out of cryo is both painless and hurtful. I am not on Preemie duty, so I actually get the whole assisted wake up procedure. The downside is that there is no physical pain to focus on, so my body immediately gravitates towards the mental pain. What initially seemed like a long gone bad dream drills into my consciousness with sharp, painful reality. The Captain and Marlon escort me to the airlock. I don't see Ally or Haru. I really would have liked to see them one last time. I barely listen when the Captain briefs the representatives of the local authorities. They ask me to confirm her story, and I do so by nodding my head. I try to drink in as much of this ship as possible. The barely audible hum of the engines, the slight vibration running through the ship caused by the life support. God help me,

I love this rustbucket. I will miss it something fierce. The Captain signs something, and without taking another look at me, she storms off. I can't blame her. She's been through enough. This whole crew has. Marlon hands me over to the authorities, and before he goes back into the ship he stops and looks at me, his expression almost apologetic. Him of all people. I don't understand anything anymore. "For what it is worth, I can understand where you came from," he mutters, his voice very quiet, very unusual for him. "I can't condone what you did, but I can understand. Take care of yourself Kevin!" He moves to close the airlock. "Take care of them Steve." I force myself to meet his eyes. "Please."
He takes a second to process what I just said, staring at me. Eventually, he nods and closes the airlock.

The officials lead me through the spaceport. As much as I hate this theme park brand of fake nostalgia, I let the stimuli wash over me. These are my people. I might not like them, but they're MY people. I am seated in some sort of car with no windows and am told to put on a blindfold. Half an hour later, the car stops and I am blindly escorted into a room. I am cuffed to a chair and the blindfold is taken off.
I am in an white, steril interrogation room, facing a big mirror. "So that's what a murderer looks like," I mutter, looking at my own reflection. The remark draws a bitter chuckle out of me.

CHAPTER XVII

For the next ten days, I spend my nights in a cell, not much smaller than my cabin on board the Dolos. During the day, nameless goons in weirdly non-descript uniforms drag me into the interrogation room, in front of that goddamn mirror. They leave me there for hours by myself, with no one to talk to but my own reflection. And let me tell you, he is a downer. When I talk to people, it's always someone different. The questions though remain the same. They all ask me what happened, why I did what I did and who I did it to. In the beginning, I don't ask questions back. I just answer, and my reflection in the mirror follows suit. With every repetition, the actions I recount feel more and more like they happened to someone else. It is on the eleventh day that things change. When they haul me into the interrogation room, there is no nervous colony rep sitting there, trying to talk slowly in a weird accent, dressed in clothes that obviously aren't his own. No, I take one look at the person who will ask the questions, and I know: today is different. He is a perfectly average man. Average height, average build, average haircut, average expression. Dressed in a simple, black uniform with an obvious plaquette on his chest. I can't read the language it is written in, but he says his name is Duprée. I sit down and watch in the mirror as Duprée sizes me up.

"Mr Ottenberg" Duprée breaks the silence and nods. Other than the interrogators before him, he does not have the weird accent. Something about how he formulates his words feels off though. As if he is constantly aware of the sounds he is producing. He articulates a bit too much. Almost as if he hadn't heard the words before. "I apologize for the delay and the repeated interrogations that you were subjected to, which lacked the proper conduct." I see myself nod in the mirror, willing to let him talk first, listening to what he has to say. As if he is reading my mind, a quick smirk touches his mouth as he continues. "Your situation is a bit of a singularity, as most of the crimes committed within the LSCT community are dealt with by the respective captains or port masters. It is also not usual for these crimes to feature any involvement of outside information." I cock my head at that phrase. "Outside information". Duprée picks up on my confused look and takes a deep breath. "I have been informed that through the interaction with the individual you know by the name "Dwight", prior to his execution, you have been informed of the existence of the Particle-Zero drive." Duprée pauses to see if I am listening. He probably thinks I am looking past him, but I focus on his figure through the mirror. "The drive from the shuttle in the container? Yes. I had a look at the plans." "I see. Well then, you are aware of the existence of space travel that is no longer in need of decades of cryo sleep and LSCT ships." I am taken aback at how matter of fact Duprée is stating this revelation.

"I am further informed that your main motivation in violently ending the existence of the individual referred to as "Dwight" was to keep the crew of your ship, as well as the rest of the LSCT trade from finding out about the Particle-Zero drive, correct?" I nod, not entirely sure where Duprée is going with that. He takes a deep breath, his eyes twitching towards the mirror. "Look, Mr Ottenberg, there is no easy way to tell you this, but I will be perfectly blunt with you. The Particle-Zero drive is already in full use throughout all human settled galaxies." Duprée watches my reaction go from confusion, to denial, to anger to bitter acceptance with an almost compassionate look in his eyes. I think of the Dolos, the crew, Ally, Haru. I think of my life, I think of my family… all the things I flushed down the drain for nothing. By the time I started my talk with Dupée, I had somewhat come to terms with the fact that I had failed in keeping my crew and my life together, but I was still holding on to hope that, at least somehow, I'd be able to salvage the status quo. Keep the Lost alive. It is weird, watching yourself react as you go through this. You've seen these emotions on other people's faces, but not yours. Never yours. "Tell me…" My voice is barely a whisper. "If that drive is already in use, why are the Lost still a thing?" Duprée looks confused. I see weird lights blink up in his eye, some sort of retina display maybe. After a second, his face lights up as he finds what he is looking for. "Ah, the Lost, right – a term used by the LSCT community to describe themselves. Please, excuse all the awkwardness of this situation. The LSCT was founded almost two millennia ago, we're trying our best to work with what we got, but a lot has been lost to time." He clears his throat. "You see Mr Ottenberg, by the time the Particle-Zero drive was ready for distribution, the LSCT ships were a huge part of the economy. You can't just shut down an industry. Further, we had created entire subcultures inside the spaceports. The logistics of integrating all these people back into society were and still are a nightmare scenario. So we kept you around. The LSCT and its spaceports are a living, breathing time capsule. It reminds us where we come from. Children being born today have no idea of the struggle that once was human conquest into space, that was human existence in its more primitive form." He smiles warmly at me as my mind struggles to make sense of the words he is throwing my way. "Again, two millennia have passed since the LSCT was introduced. Society today has as much in common with the LSCT as your "Lost" had with cavemen." "But people are spending their lives in hardship and sacrificing decades to haul ships through space," I protest, my voice refusing to carry any impact, as if the words itself cannot comprehend their meaning. "What are we hauling around in those containers then?" Duprée waits for me to calm down a bit.

"The spaceports are completely self-sufficient, so about half of the cargo hauled by the LSCT ships is actually needed for resource interaction between spaceports. The rest is artificially generated and fed into the system from the outside. A lot of people nowadays indulge in the spectacle of sending a cargo container and watching it travel through the decades. Smoke and mirrors really!" I think I should be angry at the thought of rich, stuck-up families enjoying the harsh life of the Lost for fun, but as I see my reflection trying out an angry expression I don't really feel like my heart is in it. Smoke and mirrors, he says… "In fact, the container featuring the shuttle onboard of the Dolos was entered by an especially 'inspired' individual, who thought it was a funny joke to ship a Particle-Zero drive via LSCT. Somehow, criminal elements on Dionysus Port became aware of that and tried to intervene. Hence the misfortune onboard the Dolos." "So all this… was a joke?" "A rather tasteless one, I am afraid." I chuckle. The humor sticks to the back of my throat like bile. "So what happens now?" I ask, not really expecting an answer. At this point I am only going along for the ride, not knowing if the man in the mirror should laugh or curl up in a ball on the floor and weep. Duprée shifts uneasy. "Well, you might have already gathered that we are not really adept at handling this kind of situation." I arch an eyebrow. "What situation?" "Dealing with crime and…

death. It took ten days to find someone – me – who is able to speak that ancient dialect of yours and get me here to deal with this situation – you – accordingly. But I am going to continue to be honest with you Mr Ottenberg. I might speak your dialect, and I might know how the LSCT functions, but I am utterly inept to handle the crime involved. I am merely a historian." I chuckle again. The whole situation is just too ridiculous to take seriously. "What is there to handle? I killed a man." "Technically, yes." I watch myself frown. "What's that supposed to mean?" "Well, Mr Ottenberg, in our society no one really dies anymore. We were able to resurrect your victim, and since long term and irreversible amnesia is a side effect of the "rebirth" process, we were able to re-integrate him into the LSCT community." Duprée offered me a genuine smile. "So yours was a victimless crime. And since our society doesn't really know how to handle criminals anymore, I've been instructed to clean this mess up. You are free to go Mr Ottenberg!" Duprée waves a hand towards the door. "Is the Dolos still in port?" My mind immediately goes to one, specific thing: home. Duprée frowns. "I am afraid the Dolos left this planet two days ago." These words hit me like a slap. It was one thing knowing the theory of my friends, my family being gone. It is another to have that confirmed so bluntly. Putting it from a possible scenario into a cold, hard fact. Everyone I ever cared about, could just as much have died at that moment. I lose myself in my reflection for a second, trying to cope, to find something to hang on to. I find myself grinning back at me for reasons I cannot comprehend. "Apart from that, with your memory intact, knowing what you know and your previously shown penchant to disregard laws and rules, we cannot let you back into the LSCT community. You are free to become part of the outside world though." Duprée clears his throat.
"In fact, my faculty is highly interested to meet you. We might be able to come to a mutual agreement regarding a

possible employment." "You want to study me?" I can barely contain my mockery of Duprée and his "faculty" as I fight off a giggle. "Trade one zoo in for another?" Duprée stands up and straightens out his uniform. "I know this is a lot to take in Mr Ottenberg. So I shall leave you to contemplate." He offers me another genuine smile, a business card that I do not pick up from the table and an awkward pat on the back. "It might not be yours, but this society will accept you with open arms." His work done, Duprée leaves. For several minutes I just sit there and stare at my reflection in the mirror, my mind unable to form coherent thought. Several aches stack on top of each other. The closest, the loss of friends, family, a lover, a home. Severe as it might be, it is dwarfed by the loss of a worldview and the revelation that everything I believed in, every rule I thought the world was governed by, was a farce. Worse even, the Lost are a glorified theme park. A means to pass the time for a society that had no idea of the hardship and pain and suffering the Lost were enduring.

So why in god's name can't I stop grinning… Aside from all that pain, there is fear. Fear of this society which has outlived their purpose, two thousand years between them and me. How am I supposed to handle that? I think of Duprée's caveman comparison and let out a cold, harsh laugh. I'll be just another freak show, this one more interactive than the Lost. Do I even WANT to get along with them? My mind is filled with images of my lost life. The Lost life… The Dolos, spaceports, Preemie duty, binging shows while curing a cryo hangover, XO Dickhead, the Captain, Ally, Haru… Haru. God damnit… Haru. Something gives in, and the walls of my sanity fold in on themselves as I drown in a maelstrom of impressions and memories. I cannot peel my eyes off this goddamn grin in the mirror. As I stop fighting the giggle that had been itching against the back of my throat, I think back on Duprée's words. The container being sent as a joke. And what a joke it was. The giggles turn to laughter. The laughter turns to hysterical guffaws. My whole life is a joke, so who am I to take this whole thing serious? I keep laughing until my ribs start to ache and my lungs start to burn. My eyes water and my throat turns numb. And I just keep laughing. A last bastion of rational thought in my mind briefly entertains the notion that the whole situation might not be funny at all, but that idea is quenched out quickly. Because if the joke wasn't funny, what was all of this for? My laughter travels out of the interrogation room and down the nondescript white hallway. It catches up with Duprée who is just about to leave. At the sound of it he turns around. Terrified.

DOUBLE PEPPERONI

"And that's that!" Trey's voice almost breaks with excitement as the final boss of the raid encounter finally takes a nap in the dirt.

"Damn that took a lot longer than expected!" I add as our small group of adventurers gathers around the slowly disappearing remains of the boss, waiting for the chest of loot to appear.

"Worked up quite the appetite," one of our healers remarks, and my stomach growls in agreement. How long had we been at it? I take a look at the session timer. Oh damn! We've been bashing our heads against this encounter for six hours. Definitely time to celebrate the defeat of my enemies with some doughy goodness! I open an overlay and order a pizza, pay digitally, and the system re-assures me my pie will arrive within ten minutes.

In the meantime, loot has been assigned and people start disconnecting. I exchange a couple of words with Trey, and we agree to do another run later tonight before I sign off as well.

I squint at the dim light in my apartment as I remove the visor and get off my couch. A painful knot in between my shoulder blades reminds me once more that I need to adjust my setup yet again or play less … yeah right. Who am I kidding? I find a half empty bottle of soda and down it in one go. It's flat but I don't care. Not drinking anything for six hours will do that to you. In with the new, out with the old. I take a trip to the bathroom to take care of all the pesky meat-space obligations before my food arrives.

The display next to my apartment door notifies me that the pizza bot has arrived and is currently preparing my double pepperoni pizza. I acknowledge the delivery, and within moments, a cardboard box containing my steaming hot dinner is sliding through the delivery shute. I take it and confirm the delivery once more via the display. Turning around, placing the pizza on my table, I am about to dig in when my actions are interrupted by a horrific screeching sound, followed by a couple of metallic bangs against my apartment door.

"What the—" The noise stops.

I stand in front of the door, not sure if I should open it. I try to remember the last time I was outside my apartment. When I moved here? But even then, I did the sensible thing and was on my couch. Who moves in meat-space? What year is it? 2020?

Sifting through the pile of clothes and random things next to the door, I find my old rebreather, put it on and open my apartment door. I look up and down the hallway several times before I take a step outside, looking for whatever caused the ruckus. I catch a glimpse of the pizza bot rolling around the far corner, leaving a thick, oily smear on the corridor floor that ends at my apartment door, which has several deep scratches and a couple of charming dents in it.

"Ah goddamnit!" I wheeze under my rebreather. There goes my deposit. I try to rub the back of my nose in irritation, but my fingers bounce off the mask. For a while I just stand there, looking at the door, mentally running through the steps I would have to go through to get the pizza company to pay for the damage and maybe hold on to my deposit. Right. Priorities. I go back inside my apartment, grab my cell phone and message Trey that I won't be joining him for another run tonight. Then, I stomp back out into the corridor and take a couple of photos of the damaged door, go back in, slam said door with gusto, throw the rebreather into the pile I fished it out of and slump onto my couch.

I have no desire to do this, but I cannot afford to lose my deposit, so I upload the photos I took of the door to my system, put on the visor and log in to the customer service instance.

I find myself in a traditional pizza shop as you see them in the movies. My best guess would be somewhere around the 2000s. The simulation is cheap. The world outside of the windows is blurred, the NPC customers do not have animated faces and wear the same couple sets of clothes. They do not interact with the customer, or with each other for that matter. It feels eerily like a puppet theater. The only interactive interface is the pizza baker behind the counter. He looks like the mascot on the pizza boxes.

"Helloooooo customer!" he greets me, overly loud and cheery. His face is animated, but the software is obviously outdated as his facial expressions have a weird delay and are out of sync with what he is saying. The result is that he comes across intoxicated.

I step towards the counter. "Yeah hi! I ordered a pizza with you guys and—"

"Did you enjoy your meal?" The pizza baker interrupts me.

Irritated, I try again to voice my complaint. "Yeah, as I said, I ordered a pizza with you guys and the pizza bot damaged—" - "Ten minute delivery or free!"

Oh for fuck's sake. Who still runs semi-automated customer support software? I vow to order pizza from a more contemporary place going forward and stop speaking to the rude interface as I would to another person, switching to query based input.

Let's make it as easy as possible. Simple syntax, simple sentences.

"I'd like to file a customer complaint!"

The interface smiles drunkenly at me for a moment before it's facial expression shifts to something most likely supposed to resemble earnest concern. The baker nods understandingly in an exaggerated fashion. What follows are – I can only imagine – the common FAQs to file complaints in categories.

"Are you unsatisfied with the quality of our pizza?" - "No."

"Did you receive the wrong order?" - "No"

"Did you not receive your order within ten minutes?" - "No"

"Is your complaint related to something else?" - "Yes"

"Please hold while I refer your complaint to one of our operators!" The baker's expression goes blank as he most likely refers me to the next level of customer service.

Finally someone with an actual brain to talk to. The interface starts to sing a horribly stereotypical Italian song while I wait for five minutes. Ten minutes. Twenty minutes.

Twentynine minutes and the singing finally stops, the pizza baker disappears and is replaced by a middle aged man, dressed in a red shirt bearing the pizza company's logo. The simulation's performance takes a dive. Apparently it was never built to house more than one human at the same time. Both the man behind the counter and I pause for a minute to fight a quick onset of vertigo due to the horrible framerate.

"Good day, sir. Sorry for the wait." The company representative adjusts quicker to the abysmal performance than I do. "We weren't aware anyone was still using this instance."

"Erm … its access code is on your pizza boxes," I reply sheepishly, still struggling to find my feet.

The company man cocks his head sideways. "That's irregular. Those boxes should have been renewed a while ago then." He pauses as he checks the instance's log. "So, you have a problem with your order?"

A digital display springs to life before the company man and he starts typing furiously. Without waiting for my answer he continues: "Let me just find which of our franchisées delivered your order, and I can point you in the right direction."

"Wait … right direction?" I finally adjust to the framerate and my mind starts working properly again. "You mean, you won't handle my complaint?"

The company man stops and looks at me like I just asked something incredibly stupid. "Of course not. Our franchisées operate completely autonomously from the main franchise."

I take a deep breath because I can feel the situation getting away from me. "Listen man, I didn't get a wrong pizza or something, the pizza bot scratched my apartment door and I just want someone to pay for the damage."

He looks at me with an empty expression. "I am sure our franchisée will gladly address your complaint. Here is the digital address of the franchisée in question." An address is pushed into my inbox.

I feel like I am being handled. I don't like being handled. "Can't you just talk to—"

"No we can't, I am sorry." Now it is the company guy who interrupts me, flashing me a shit eating grin. "Have a nice day!"

And with that I am thrown out of the instance without any warning and find myself back on my couch, disoriented and a bit motion sick. I am definitely not going to order pizza from that franchise ever again! Taking a few moments to get my bearings, I queue up the login the company prick gave me and reconnect to the net.

I find myself in a default waiting room. A cheap rendering of an apartment hallway with several doors. A common lobby for small one-person businesses, usually shared by a couple of freelancers to save on hosting fees. I check the doors until I find the apartment corresponding to the pizza franchisée and knock. No response. I knock a second time. A third time.

By the time I have to knock a fourth time, I queue up a priority notification script and push it alongside my contact request. That way, it will be next to impossible for the guy to ignore me, and wouldn't you know it, it works. The door opens and I am faced with an abstract matrix. That is odd. Only digital natives appear like that in simulations, and as far as I am aware, natives can't be franchisées of meat-space businesses. It is a whole "liability" thing. Outdated if you ask me, but it is the law. I start to feel tense.

"Erm … are you," I check the information given to me by the pizza man, "Norman Bytes?" I feel stupid the second the words leave my lips. I hadn't checked the name until now. An obvious fake name. The data matrix laughs at me. A weird digitized laugh.

"I use that alias, yes. What do you want?" Norman or whatever he is called is a matrix of few words apparently.

"I got this address from the pizza company. Your bot scratched my door." I get right to the point.

The matrix takes a second to respond. "Tough shit buddy. Not my problem."

"You are the franchisée. And according to the company you have to—" I try to argue, but again – and this seems to become a pattern today – I am cut off.

"No I am not, and no I don't have to do anything," the matrix states bluntly. Obviously I look confused because after a moment Norman sighs and starts to explain. "Look, you know as a matrix I can't be a franchisée. I took that job when I still had my body. But it got outsourced when I went full digital. Whoever scratched your door wasn't me bro!"

Now it is my turn to sigh. "How can you go digital when

you have running contracts in meat-space?"

"Not my choice bro." Am I imagining it or is there a hint of sadness in Norman's voice? "Foreclosure. Never even got to know who took over my body. They just tossed me into digital because I couldn't pay up. Nowadays I crunch numbers for a chain of retail stores." He pauses for a second. "Might even be able to buy a body again in a decade or two."

I've heard of cases like that. It is common practice. People who can't afford to pay their bills are forced to go digital, because their body is the last thing of value they can sell. I remember the sum of my deposit and have to swallow a quickly forming knot at the back of my throat. People who can't afford to pay their bills … or refund their deposits.

"Any idea who knows who's running your body nowadays?" I'm grasping at straws at this point. Norman is silent for a moment. "Check the local branch of the tax office. It was an official auction. As far as I know, there should be a trail."

I rub the back of my nose. Both in digital as well as in meat-space under my visor.

"I appreciate it man. You know … not a lot but …"

"Yeah bro, I feel you. Hope you figure it out!"

And with that, I leave digital and sit up on my couch in my apartment. Querying the tax office of all things. That will take fucking forever.

By the time I figure out how to address my request and who to send it to, I get an email from my landlord. Of course a maintenance bot has come by my apartment door and noticed the damage, immediately notifying him of the scratches and dents on the door. The email informs me that my deposit is nullified. I am in the middle of trying to explain to my landlord that I am currently tracking down the person responsible for the damage when I get another email from the tax office. I open it and my blood runs cold.

It reads:

"We have filed your query accordingly. Unfortunately we have to inform you that the asset in question has reportedly perished as of twenty-five hours ago. The proprietor of the asset has nullified all existing business dealings concerning the asset and has opted to go back to digital native status."

The fucker knew full well I was going to fine them for damaging my door, so they retreated into digital. No way I will get the money back from them for fixing my door.

I look around my apartment and take a deep breath. My lease is running out in a couple of months, so until then, I won't have a problem with not getting my deposit back. I won't be able to afford a new place though …

I sit back on my couch and put on the visor, shooting Trey a message.

"Might go digital native in a couple of months. Let's make the most of it for now, care for another run?"

A COUPLE OF WORDS

Tales of Yesterday's Tomorrow is a collection (or anthology if you're feeling pretentious) of my previous two science fiction novellas as well as one published and one (until now) unpublished short story.

I haven't really done physical book releases yet. There was an attempt at a physical release of The Foreign Effect's original version, but I like to pretend that catastrophe of a version never existed… As someone who prefers physical books over e-books (I am a science fiction writer, naturally progress scares me), a big part of wanting to do this collection of stories is the creation of a physical thing. You can't borrow an e-book from a friend, you can't smell the paper, you can't bend the back and make the book your own. And most importantly, you can't prop up a dodgy table leg with an e-book. You can with a physical copy. So, may all your tables always be steadfast!

ABOUT THE AUTHOR

Rich Winterstetter always liked to tell stories and continues to do so no matter the format or genre. His parents made the mistake of raising him with Star Wars and Star Trek and therefore ruined him for more traditional fiction.

When he isn't writing, Rich likes to spend his time in other people's universes. He is a big tabletop and video-gaming nerd and occasionally even posts something on his blog over at rich-winterstetter.com. The 34-year-old lives in Bavaria, Germany with an imaginary wombat called Bruce and too many distractions from writing.